W9-APC-940

CHIMA

Yannick Grotholt – Writer
Comicon – Artist

PAPERCUT乙™

New York

LEGO® CHIMA Graphic Novels Available from PAPERCUTZ™

LEGO
LEGENDS OF
CHIMA
ALL-NEW GRAPHIC NOVEL SERIES!
HIGH RISK!
YANNICK GROTHOLT
COMICON
PAPERCUTZ

Graphic Novel #1
"High Risk!"

LEGO
LEGENDS OF
CHIMA
THE RIGHT DECISION
YANNICK GROTHOLT
COMICON
PAPERCUTZ

Graphic Novel #2
"The Right Decision"

LEGO
LEGENDS OF
CHIMA
CHI QUEST!
YANNICK GROTHOLT
COMICON
PAPERCUTZ

Graphic Novel #3
"CHI Quest!"

LEGO
LEGENDS OF
CHIMA
THE POWER OF FIRE CHI
YANNICK GROTHOLT
COMICON
PAPERCUTZ

Graphic Novel #4
"The Power of Fire CHI"

LEGENDS OF CHIMA
#4 "The Power of Fire CHI"

Yannick Grotholt – Writer
Comicon – Artist
(Miguel Sanchez – Pencils
Marc Alberich – Inks
Oriol San Julian – Color
Bryan Senka – Letterer
Noah Sharma – Editorial Intern
Jeff Whitman – Production Coordinator
Michael Petranek – Editor
Jim Salicrup
Editor-in-Chief

ISBN: 978-1-62991-155-7 paperback edition
ISBN: 978-1-62991-156-4 hardcover edition

FSC
www.fsc.org
MIX
Paper from responsible sources
FSC® C006398

Printed in Hong Kong
May 2015 by Asia One Printing LTD
13/F Asia One Tower
8 Fung Yip St, Chaiwan
Hong Kong

LEGO LEGENDS OF CHIMA graphic novels are available for $7.99 in paperback, $12.99 hardcover. Available from booksellers everywhere. You can also order online from Papercutz.com. Or call 1-800-886-1223, Monday through Friday, 9-5 EST. MC, Visa, and AmEx accepted. To order by mail, please add $4.00 for postage and handling for first book ordered, $1.00 for each additional book and make check payable to NBM Publishing. Send to: Papercutz, 160 Broadway, Suite 700, East Wing, New York, NY 10038.

LEGO LEGENDS OF CHIMA graphic novels are also available digitally wherever e-books are sold.

Papercutz.com

Papercutz books may be purchased for business or promotional use. For information on bulk purchases please contact Macmillan Corporate and Premium Sales Department at (800) 221-7945 x5442.

Distributed by Macmillan
Second Papercutz Printing

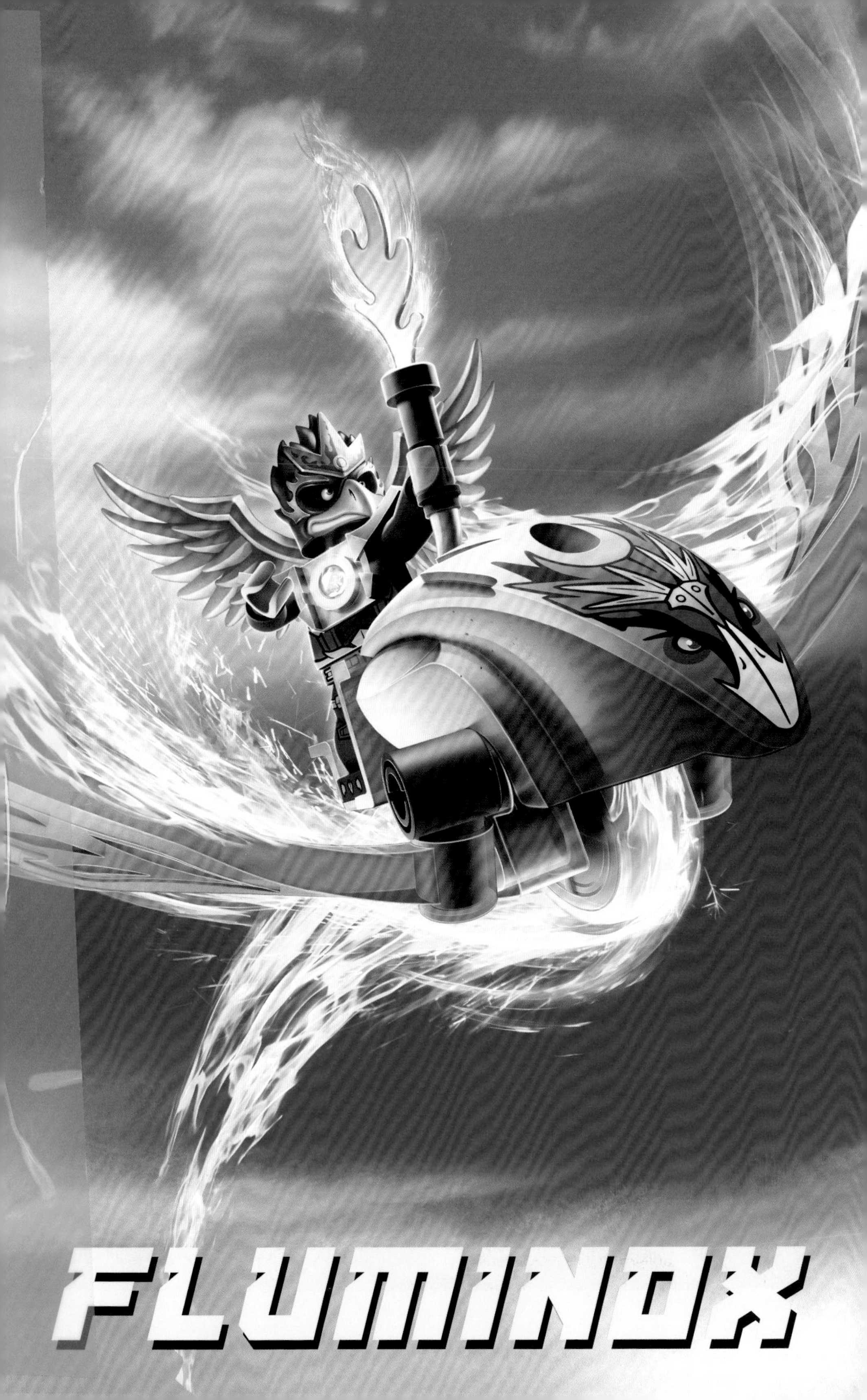
FLUMINOX

The POWER of FIRE CHI

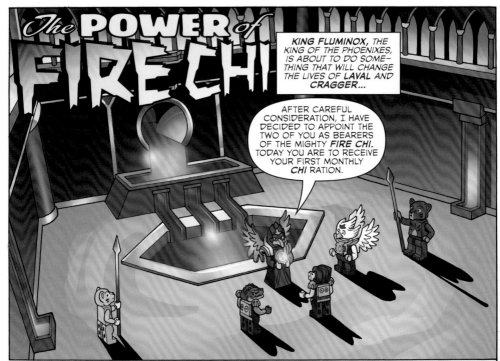

KING FLUMINOX, THE KING OF THE PHOENIXES, IS ABOUT TO DO SOMETHING THAT WILL CHANGE THE LIVES OF LAVAL AND CRAGGER...

AFTER CAREFUL CONSIDERATION, I HAVE DECIDED TO APPOINT THE TWO OF YOU AS BEARERS OF THE MIGHTY FIRE CHI. TODAY YOU ARE TO RECEIVE YOUR FIRST MONTHLY CHI RATION.

USE IT WELL AND--

--USE IT WISELY. MY FATHER SAYS THAT, TOO.

DOES HE REALLY? I'LL SAVE MYSELF THE SACRED WORDS IN FUTURE.

THE PHOENIXES CONSIDER IT A GREAT INSULT IF YOU INTERRUPT THEM.

ROYAL ETIQUETTE HAS NEVER BEEN LAVAL'S STRONG POINT...

LUCKILY, KING FLUMINOX IS IN A GOOD MOOD AND DESPITE LAVAL'S FAUX PAS, HE PRESENTS THE FIRE CHI TO THE YOUNG WARRIORS...

THINGS ARE GOING TO GET VERY HOT FOR THE SABER-TOOTH TIGERS!

YOU BET THEY ARE!

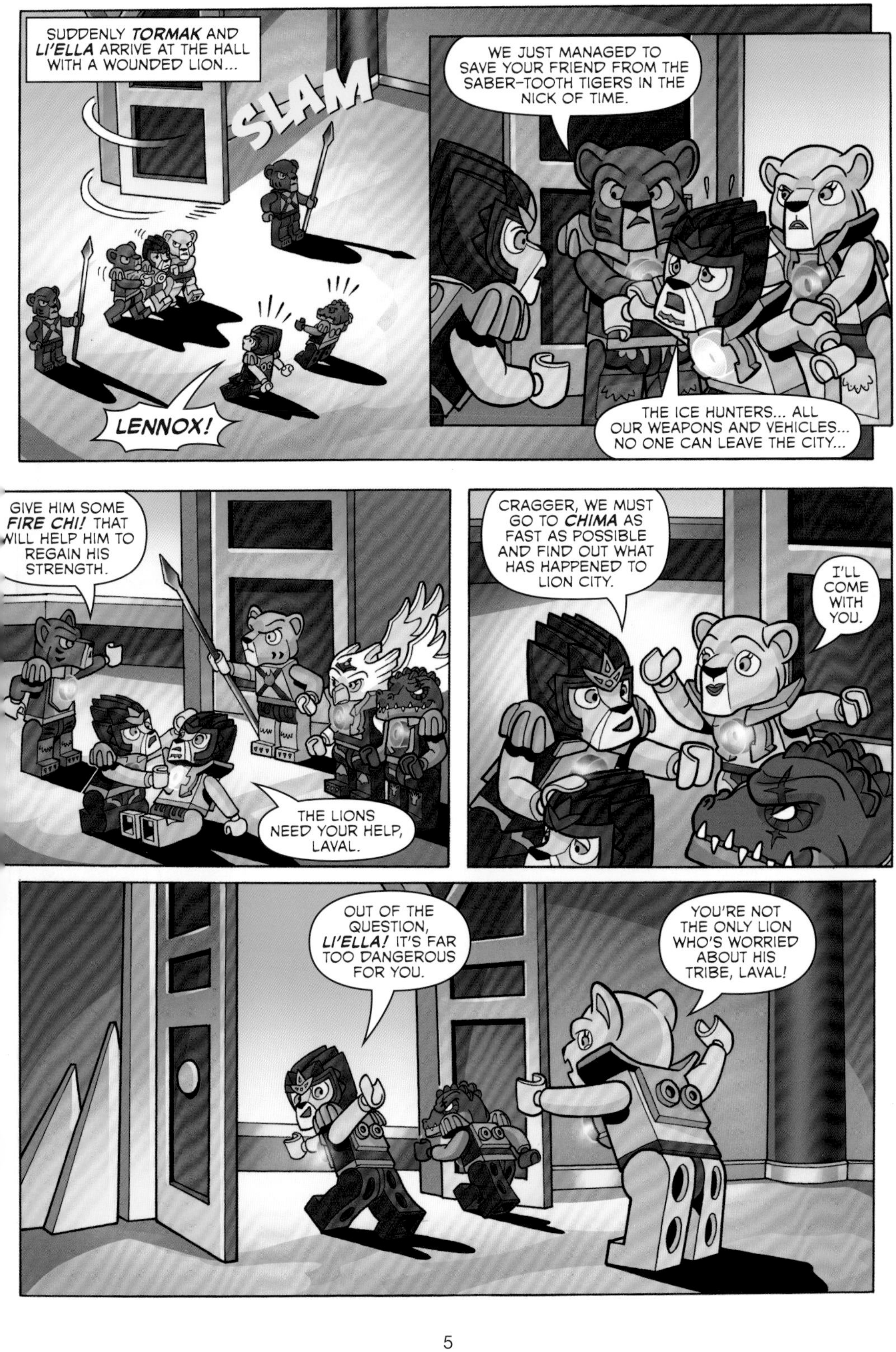

SUDDENLY TORMAK AND LI'ELLA ARRIVE AT THE HALL WITH A WOUNDED LION...
SLAM
LENNOX!
WE JUST MANAGED TO SAVE YOUR FRIEND FROM THE SABER-TOOTH TIGERS IN THE NICK OF TIME.
THE ICE HUNTERS... ALL OUR WEAPONS AND VEHICLES... NO ONE CAN LEAVE THE CITY...
GIVE HIM SOME FIRE CHI! THAT WILL HELP HIM TO REGAIN HIS STRENGTH.
THE LIONS NEED YOUR HELP, LAVAL.
CRAGGER, WE MUST GO TO CHIMA AS FAST AS POSSIBLE AND FIND OUT WHAT HAS HAPPENED TO LION CITY.
I'LL COME WITH YOU.
OUT OF THE QUESTION, LI'ELLA! IT'S FAR TOO DANGEROUS FOR YOU.
YOU'RE NOT THE ONLY LION WHO'S WORRIED ABOUT HIS TRIBE, LAVAL!

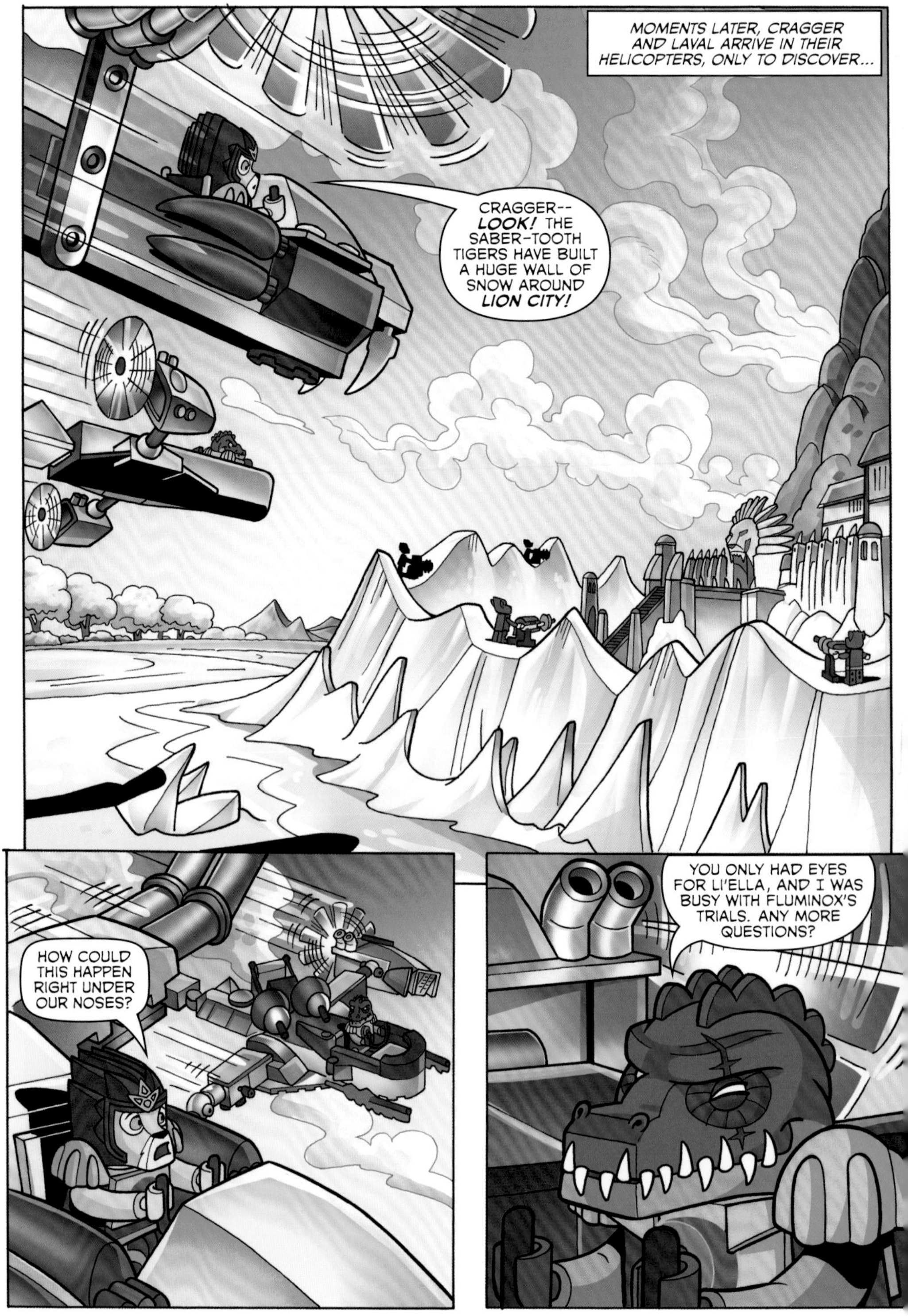
MOMENTS LATER, CRAGGER AND LAVAL ARRIVE IN THEIR HELICOPTERS, ONLY TO DISCOVER...
CRAGGER-- LOOK! THE SABER-TOOTH TIGERS HAVE BUILT A HUGE WALL OF SNOW AROUND LION CITY!
HOW COULD THIS HAPPEN RIGHT UNDER OUR NOSES?
YOU ONLY HAD EYES FOR LI'ELLA, AND I WAS BUSY WITH FLUMINOX'S TRIALS. ANY MORE QUESTIONS?

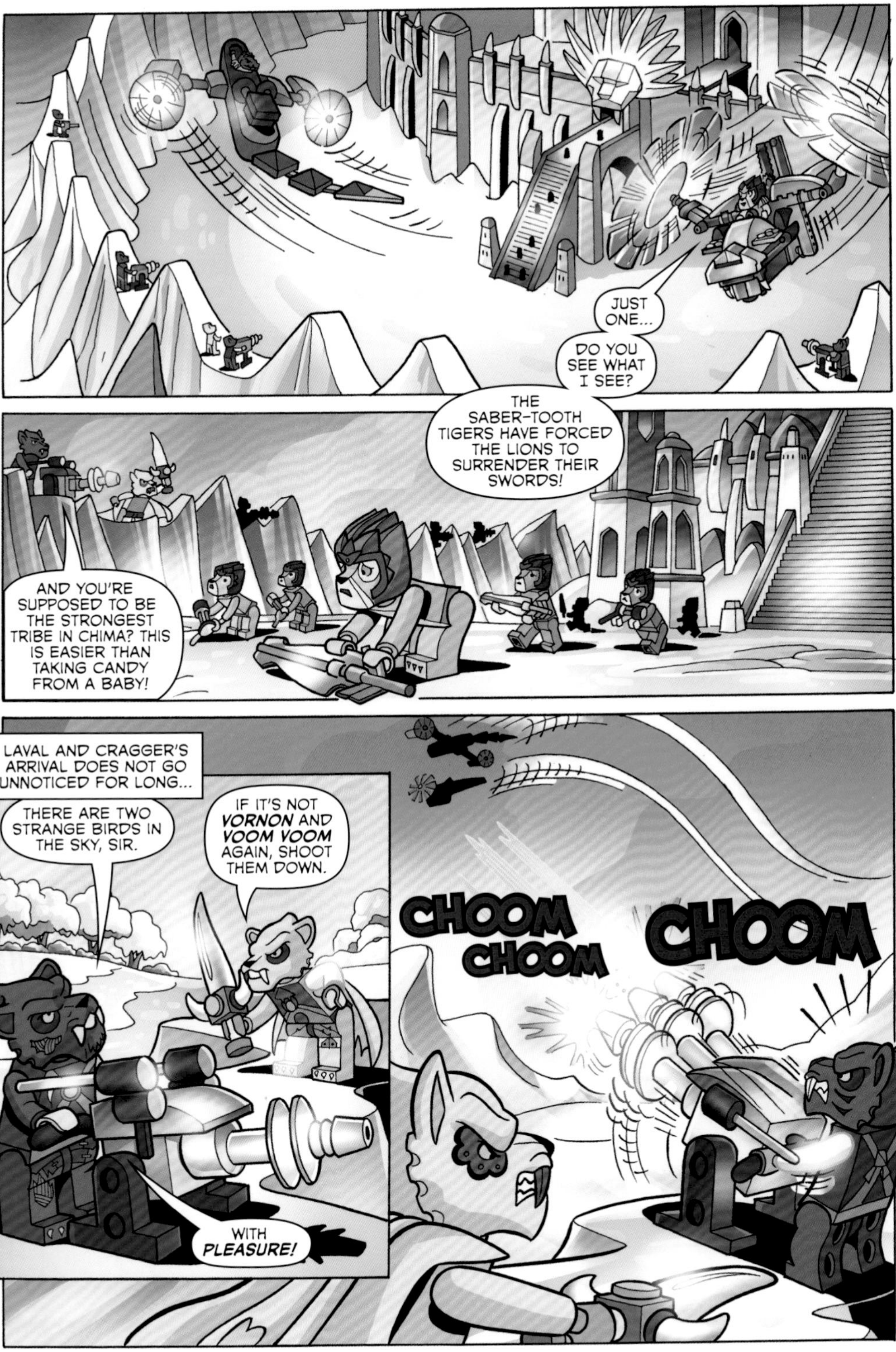
JUST ONE...
DO YOU SEE WHAT I SEE?
THE SABER-TOOTH TIGERS HAVE FORCED THE LIONS TO SURRENDER THEIR SWORDS!
AND YOU'RE SUPPOSED TO BE THE STRONGEST TRIBE IN CHIMA? THIS IS EASIER THAN TAKING CANDY FROM A BABY!
LAVAL AND CRAGGER'S ARRIVAL DOES NOT GO UNNOTICED FOR LONG...
THERE ARE TWO STRANGE BIRDS IN THE SKY, SIR.
IF IT'S NOT *VORNON* AND *VOOM VOOM* AGAIN, SHOOT THEM DOWN.
WITH *PLEASURE!*
CHOOM CHOOM
CHOOM

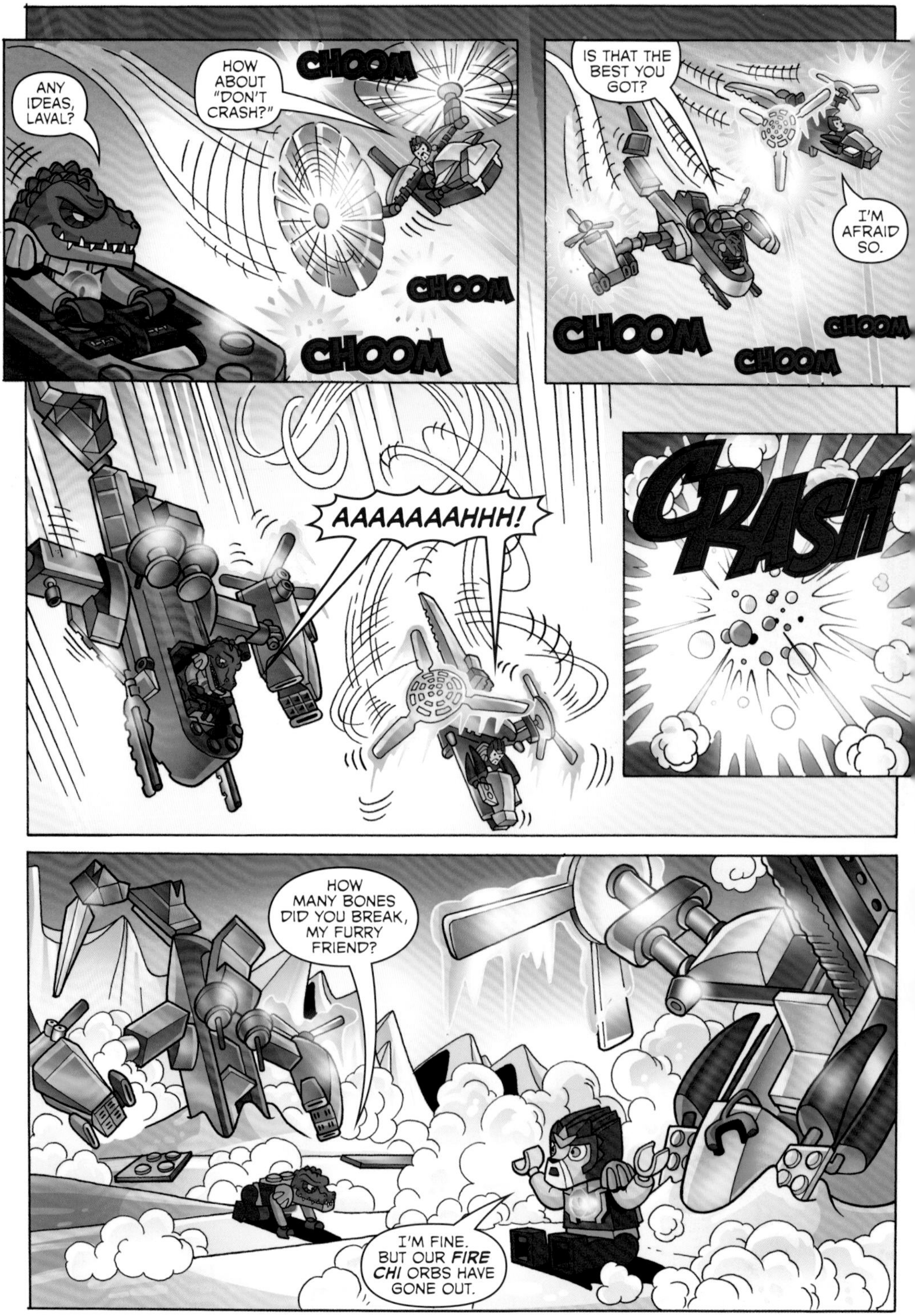
ANY IDEAS, LAVAL?
HOW ABOUT "DON'T CRASH?"
CHOOM
CHOOM
CHOOM
IS THAT THE BEST YOU GOT?
I'M AFRAID SO.
CHOOM
CHOOM
CHOOM
AAAAAAAHHH!
CRASH
HOW MANY BONES DID YOU BREAK, MY FURRY FRIEND?
I'M FINE. BUT OUR ***FIRE CHI*** ORBS HAVE GONE OUT.

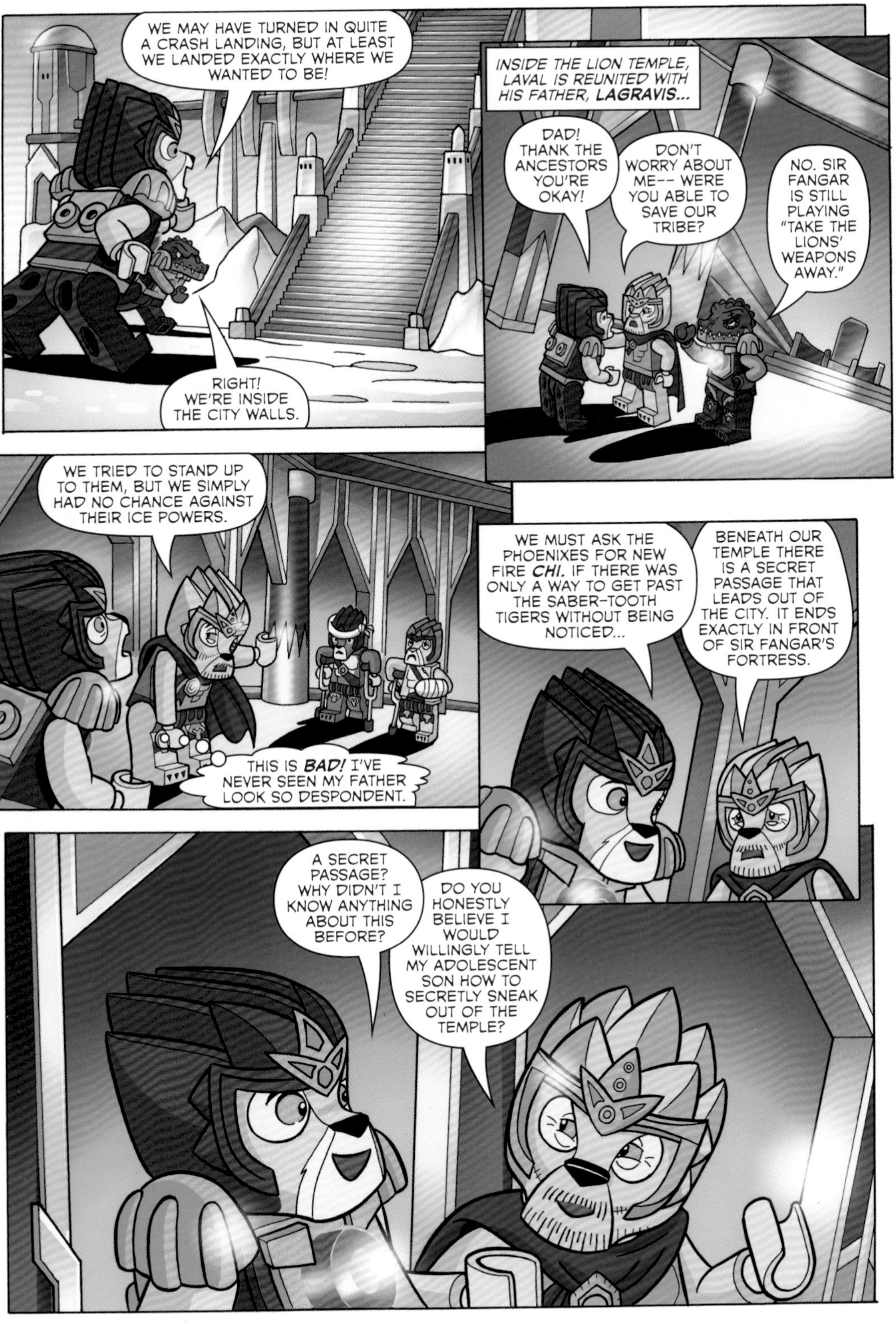
WE MAY HAVE TURNED IN QUITE A CRASH LANDING, BUT AT LEAST WE LANDED EXACTLY WHERE WE WANTED TO BE!
RIGHT! WE'RE INSIDE THE CITY WALLS.
INSIDE THE LION TEMPLE, LAVAL IS REUNITED WITH HIS FATHER, LAGRAVIS...
DAD! THANK THE ANCESTORS YOU'RE OKAY!
DON'T WORRY ABOUT ME-- WERE YOU ABLE TO SAVE OUR TRIBE?
NO. SIR FANGAR IS STILL PLAYING "TAKE THE LIONS' WEAPONS AWAY."
WE TRIED TO STAND UP TO THEM, BUT WE SIMPLY HAD NO CHANCE AGAINST THEIR ICE POWERS.
THIS IS BAD! I'VE NEVER SEEN MY FATHER LOOK SO DESPONDENT.
WE MUST ASK THE PHOENIXES FOR NEW FIRE CHI. IF THERE WAS ONLY A WAY TO GET PAST THE SABER-TOOTH TIGERS WITHOUT BEING NOTICED...
BENEATH OUR TEMPLE THERE IS A SECRET PASSAGE THAT LEADS OUT OF THE CITY. IT ENDS EXACTLY IN FRONT OF SIR FANGAR'S FORTRESS.
A SECRET PASSAGE? WHY DIDN'T I KNOW ANYTHING ABOUT THIS BEFORE?
DO YOU HONESTLY BELIEVE I WOULD WILLINGLY TELL MY ADOLESCENT SON HOW TO SECRETLY SNEAK OUT OF THE TEMPLE?

HOURS LATER...

HURRY UP, LAVAL. THERE'S NO TIME TO LOSE!

I JUST CAN'T BELIEVE THIS SECRET TUNNEL EXISTS!

I WONDER WHAT OTHER SECRETS MY FATHER IS KEEPING FROM ME.

I WONDER IF LAGRAVIS ALSO KNEW ABOUT THIS!

WHAT--?

SEE FOR YOUR-SELF!

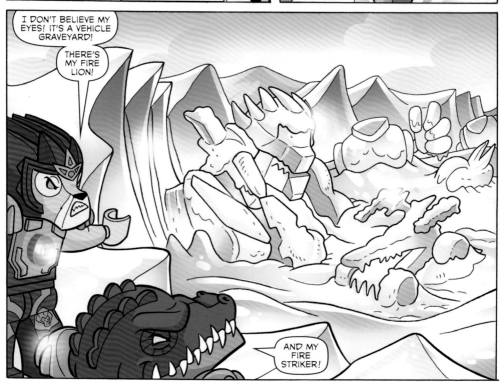

I DON'T BELIEVE MY EYES! IT'S A VEHICLE GRAVEYARD!

THERE'S MY FIRE LION!

AND MY FIRE STRIKER!

10

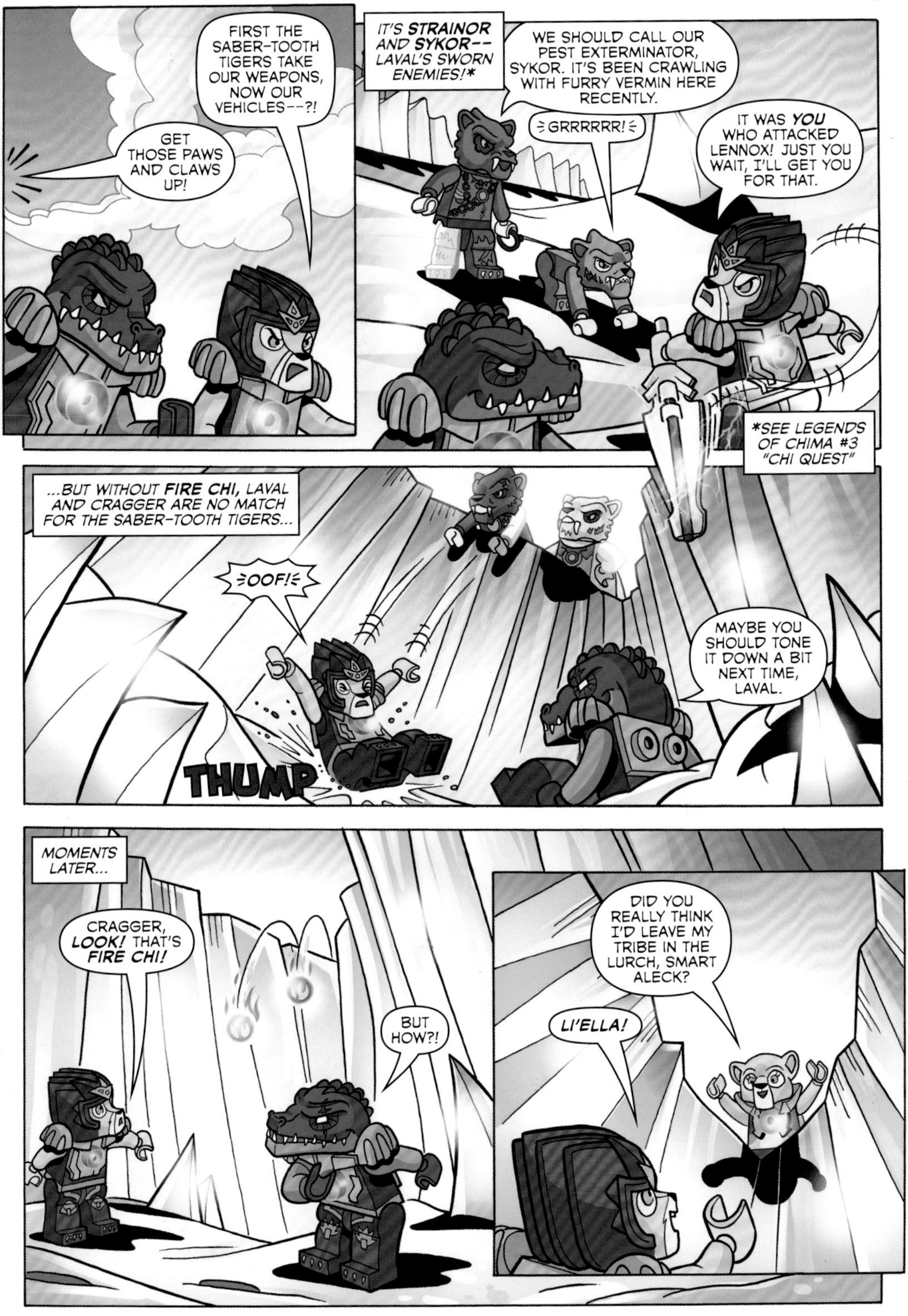

FIRST THE SABER-TOOTH TIGERS TAKE OUR WEAPONS, NOW OUR VEHICLES--?!
GET THOSE PAWS AND CLAWS UP!
IT'S STRAINOR AND SYKOR-- LAVAL'S SWORN ENEMIES!*
WE SHOULD CALL OUR PEST EXTERMINATOR, SYKOR. IT'S BEEN CRAWLING WITH FURRY VERMIN HERE RECENTLY.
GRRRRRR!
IT WAS YOU WHO ATTACKED LENNOX! JUST YOU WAIT, I'LL GET YOU FOR THAT.
*SEE LEGENDS OF CHIMA #3 "CHI QUEST"
...BUT WITHOUT FIRE CHI, LAVAL AND CRAGGER ARE NO MATCH FOR THE SABER-TOOTH TIGERS...
OOF!
THUMP
MAYBE YOU SHOULD TONE IT DOWN A BIT NEXT TIME, LAVAL.
MOMENTS LATER...
CRAGGER, LOOK! THAT'S FIRE CHI!
BUT HOW?!
DID YOU REALLY THINK I'D LEAVE MY TRIBE IN THE LURCH, SMART ALECK?
LI'ELLA!

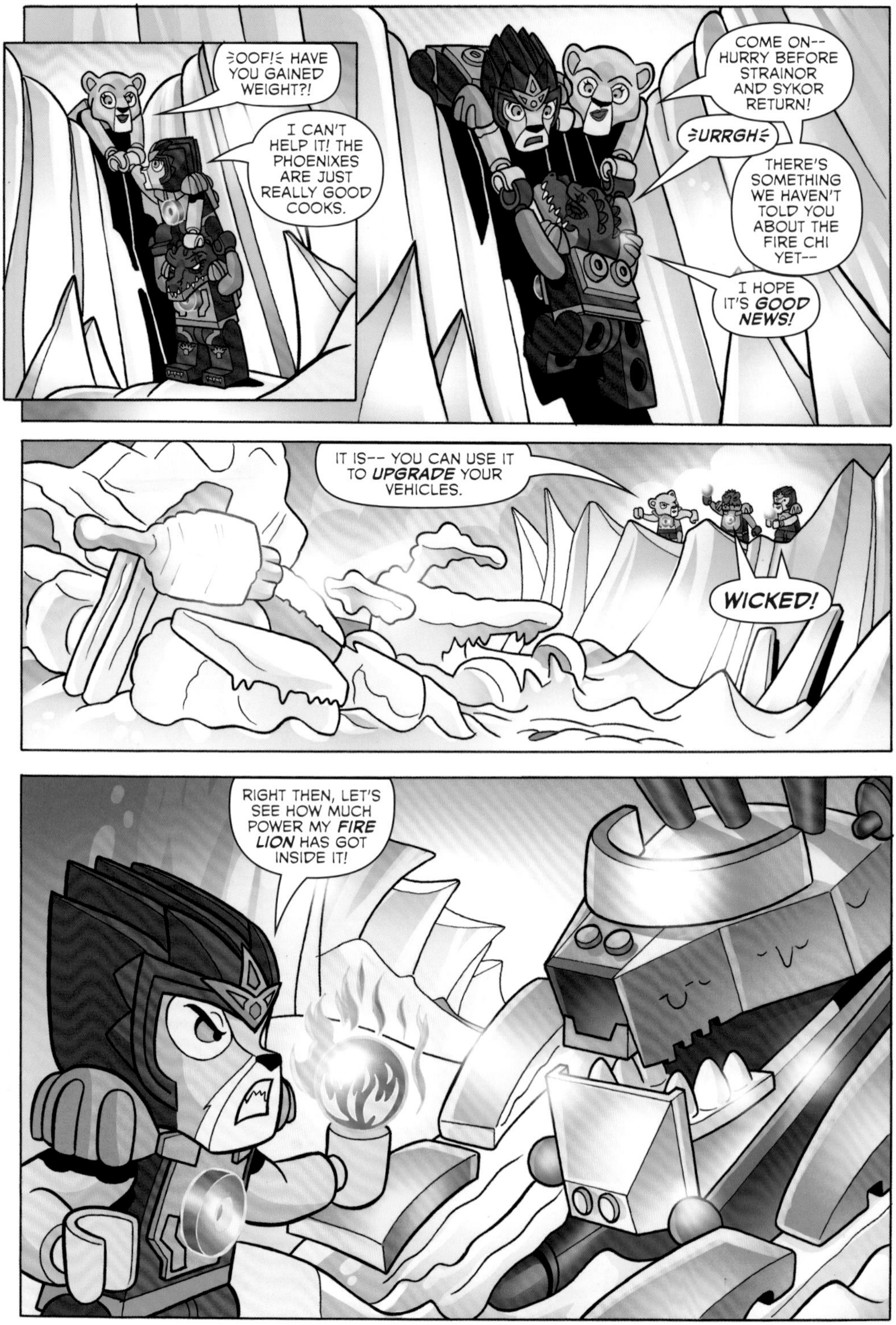
≶OOF!≶ HAVE YOU GAINED WEIGHT?!
I CAN'T HELP IT! THE PHOENIXES ARE JUST REALLY GOOD COOKS.
COME ON-- HURRY BEFORE STRAINOR AND SYKOR RETURN!
≶URRGH≶
THERE'S SOMETHING WE HAVEN'T TOLD YOU ABOUT THE FIRE CHI YET--
I HOPE IT'S GOOD NEWS!
IT IS-- YOU CAN USE IT TO UPGRADE YOUR VEHICLES.
WICKED!
RIGHT THEN, LET'S SEE HOW MUCH POWER MY FIRE LION HAS GOT INSIDE IT!

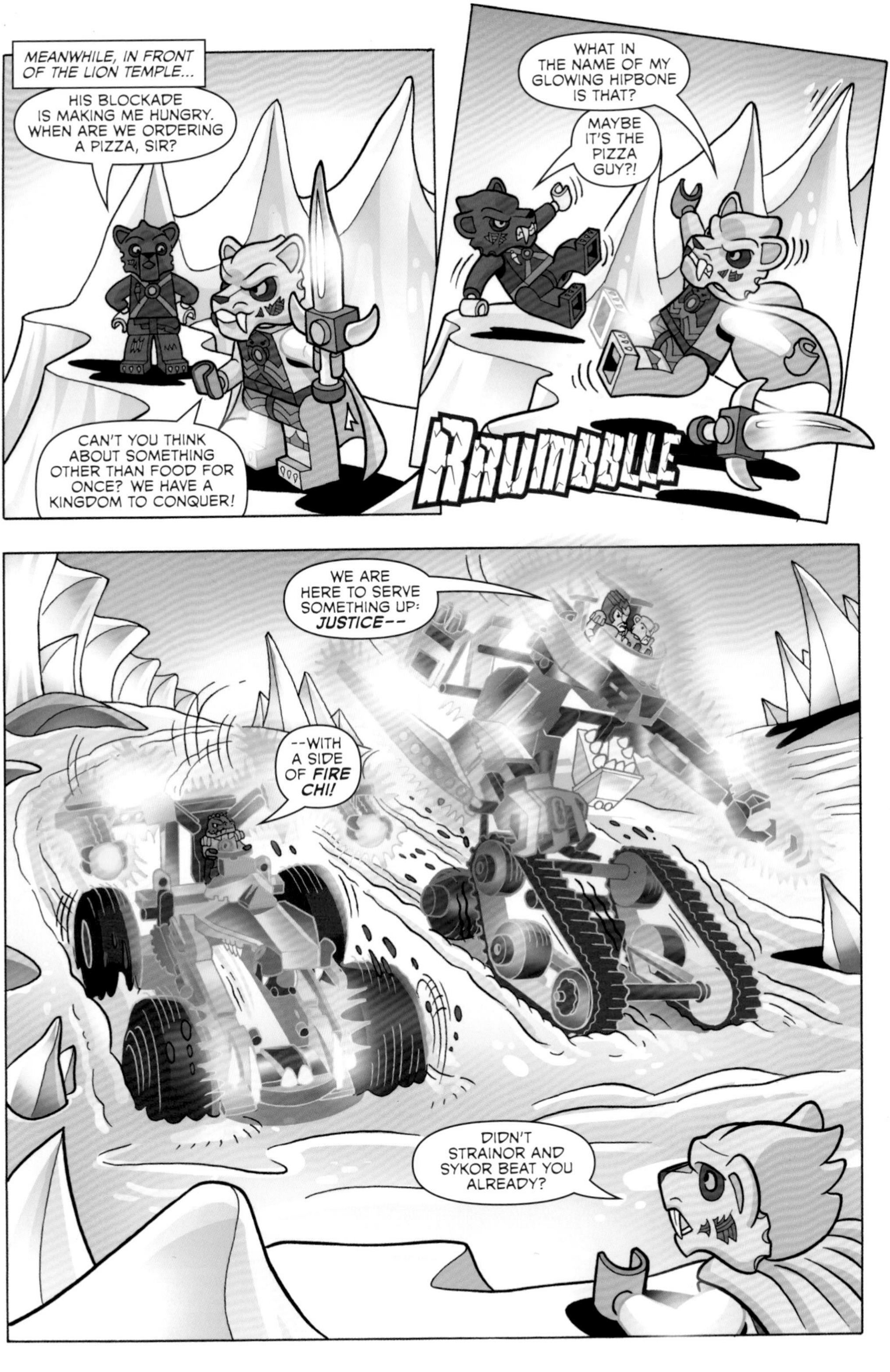
MEANWHILE, IN FRONT OF THE LION TEMPLE...
HIS BLOCKADE IS MAKING ME HUNGRY. WHEN ARE WE ORDERING A PIZZA, SIR?
CAN'T YOU THINK ABOUT SOMETHING OTHER THAN FOOD FOR ONCE? WE HAVE A KINGDOM TO CONQUER!
WHAT IN THE NAME OF MY GLOWING HIPBONE IS THAT?
MAYBE IT'S THE PIZZA GUY?!
BRRUMBBLLE
WE ARE HERE TO SERVE SOMETHING UP: JUSTICE--
--WITH A SIDE OF FIRE CHI!
DIDN'T STRAINOR AND SYKOR BEAT YOU ALREADY?

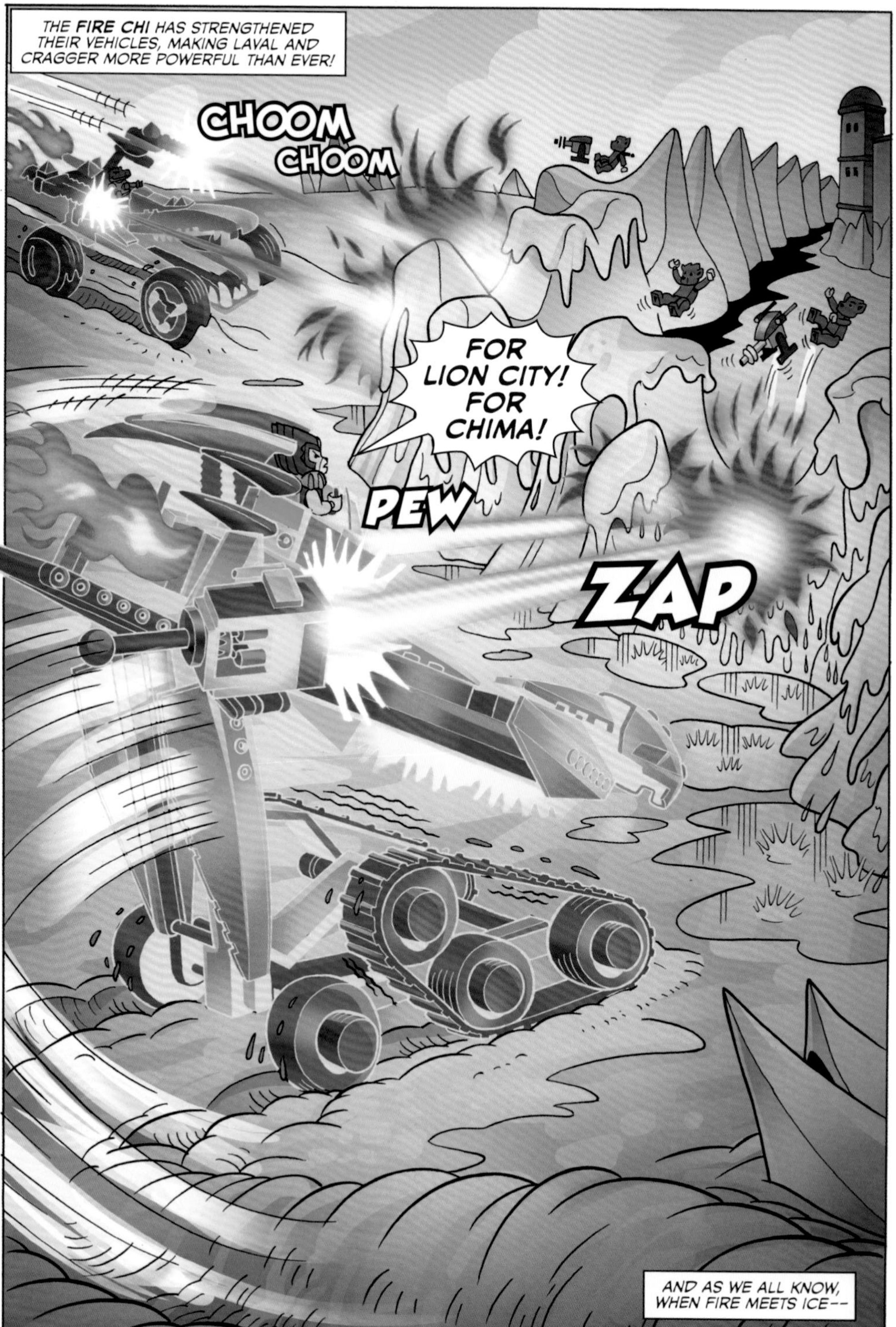
THE **FIRE CHI** HAS STRENGTHENED THEIR VEHICLES, MAKING LAVAL AND CRAGGER MORE POWERFUL THAN EVER!
CHOOM
CHOOM
FOR LION CITY! FOR CHIMA!
PEW
ZAP
AND AS WE ALL KNOW, WHEN FIRE MEETS ICE--

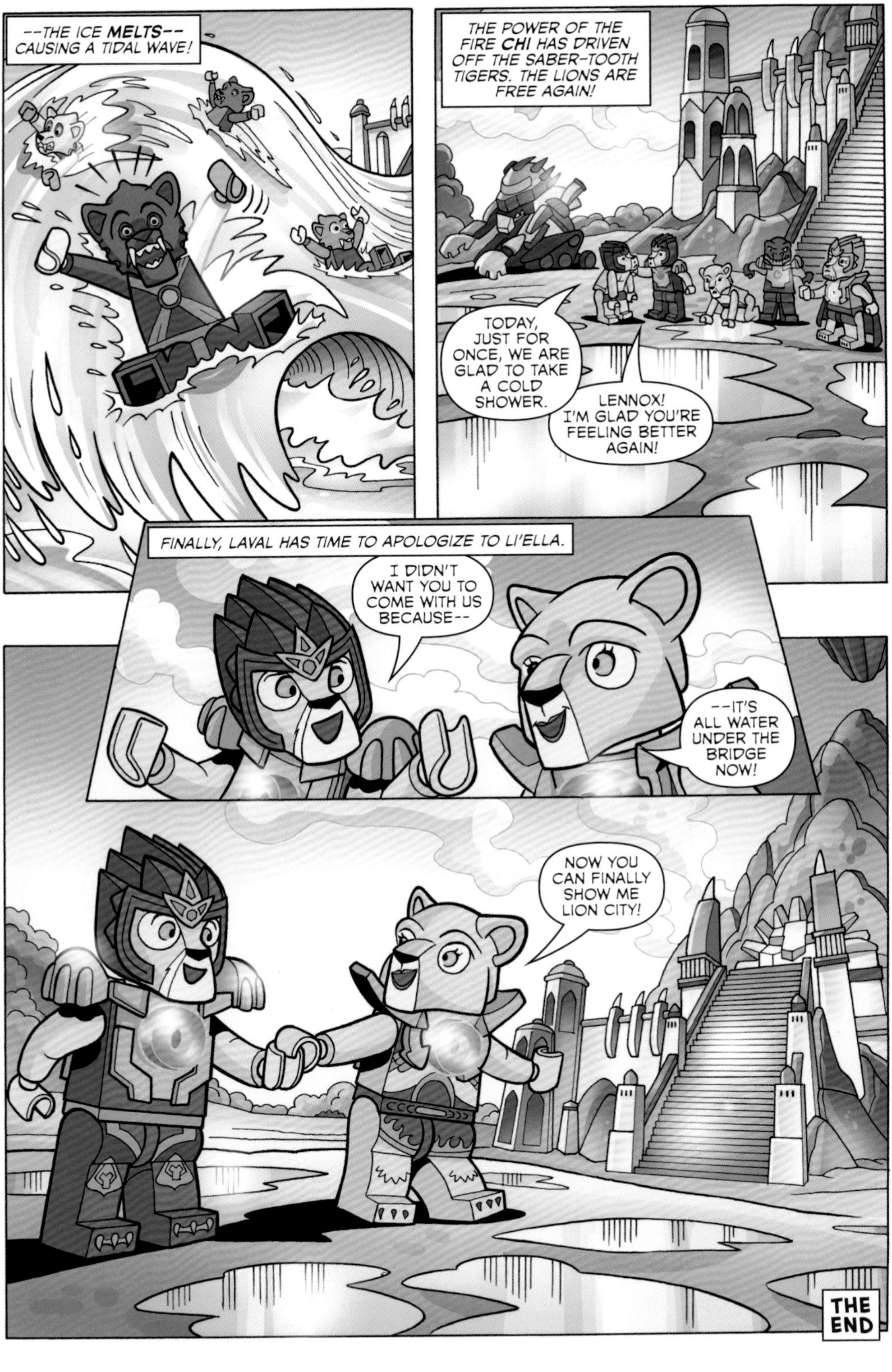
--THE ICE MELTS-- CAUSING A TIDAL WAVE!
THE POWER OF THE FIRE CHI HAS DRIVEN OFF THE SABER-TOOTH TIGERS. THE LIONS ARE FREE AGAIN!
TODAY, JUST FOR ONCE, WE ARE GLAD TO TAKE A COLD SHOWER.
LENNOX! I'M GLAD YOU'RE FEELING BETTER AGAIN!
FINALLY, LAVAL HAS TIME TO APOLOGIZE TO LI'ELLA.
I DIDN'T WANT YOU TO COME WITH US BECAUSE--
--IT'S ALL WATER UNDER THE BRIDGE NOW!
NOW YOU CAN FINALLY SHOW ME LION CITY!
THE END

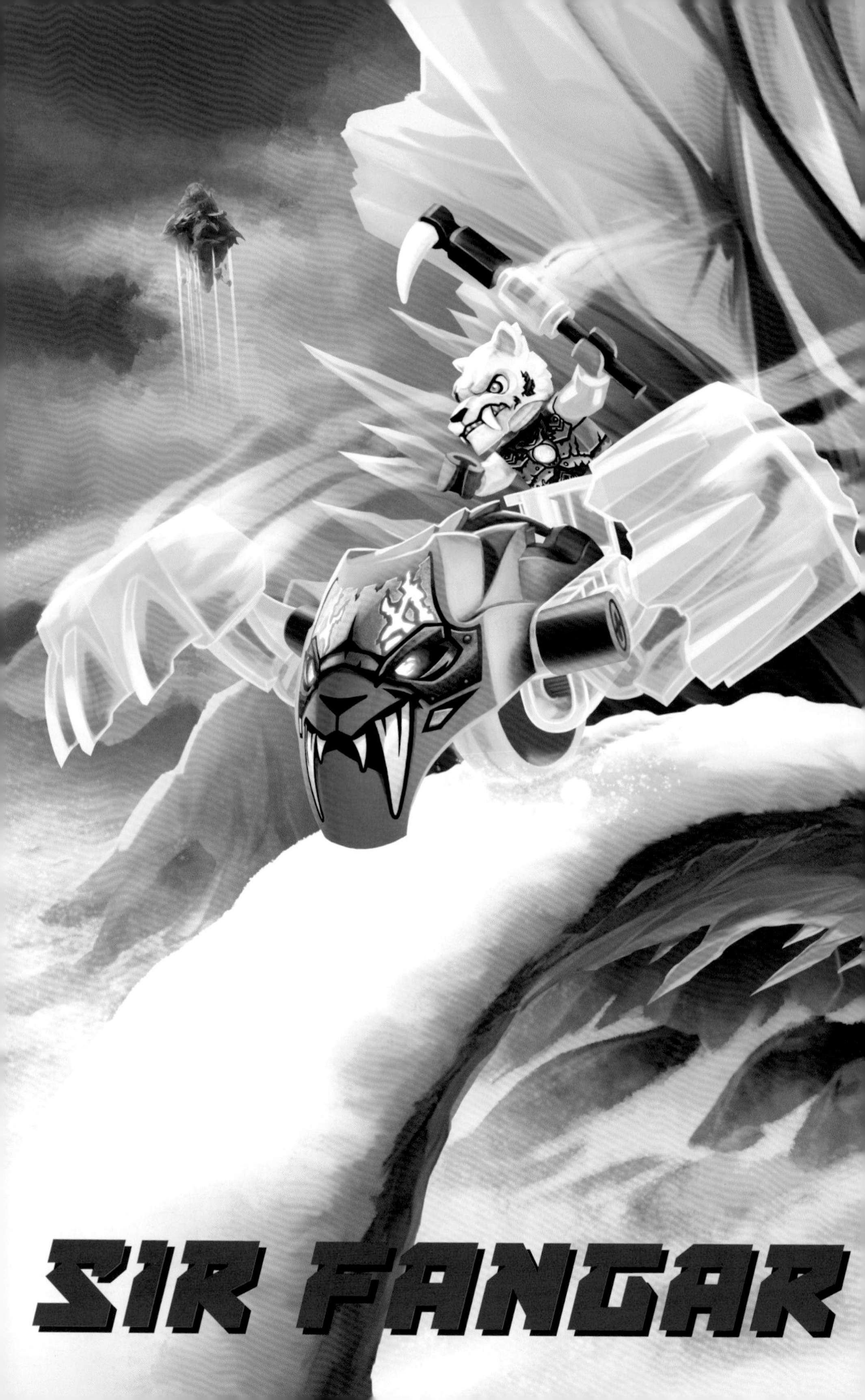

SIR FANGAR

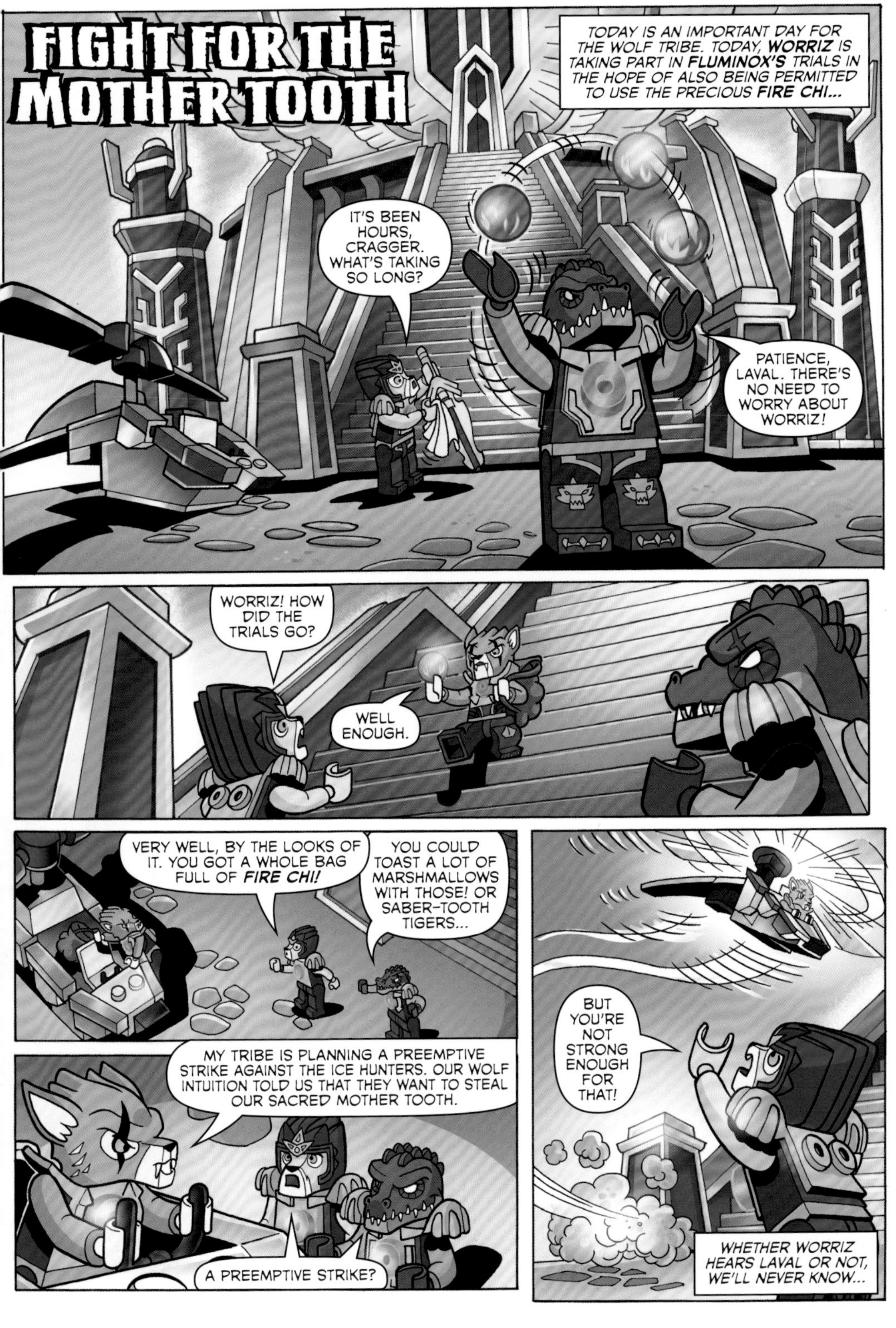
FIGHT FOR THE MOTHER TOOTH
TODAY IS AN IMPORTANT DAY FOR THE WOLF TRIBE. TODAY, WORRIZ IS TAKING PART IN FLUMINOX'S TRIALS IN THE HOPE OF ALSO BEING PERMITTED TO USE THE PRECIOUS FIRE CHI...
IT'S BEEN HOURS, CRAGGER. WHAT'S TAKING SO LONG?
PATIENCE, LAVAL. THERE'S NO NEED TO WORRY ABOUT WORRIZ!
WORRIZ! HOW DID THE TRIALS GO?
WELL ENOUGH.
VERY WELL, BY THE LOOKS OF IT. YOU GOT A WHOLE BAG FULL OF FIRE CHI!
YOU COULD TOAST A LOT OF MARSHMALLOWS WITH THOSE! OR SABER-TOOTH TIGERS...
MY TRIBE IS PLANNING A PREEMPTIVE STRIKE AGAINST THE ICE HUNTERS. OUR WOLF INTUITION TOLD US THAT THEY WANT TO STEAL OUR SACRED MOTHER TOOTH.
A PREEMPTIVE STRIKE?
BUT YOU'RE NOT STRONG ENOUGH FOR THAT!
WHETHER WORRIZ HEARS LAVAL OR NOT, WE'LL NEVER KNOW...

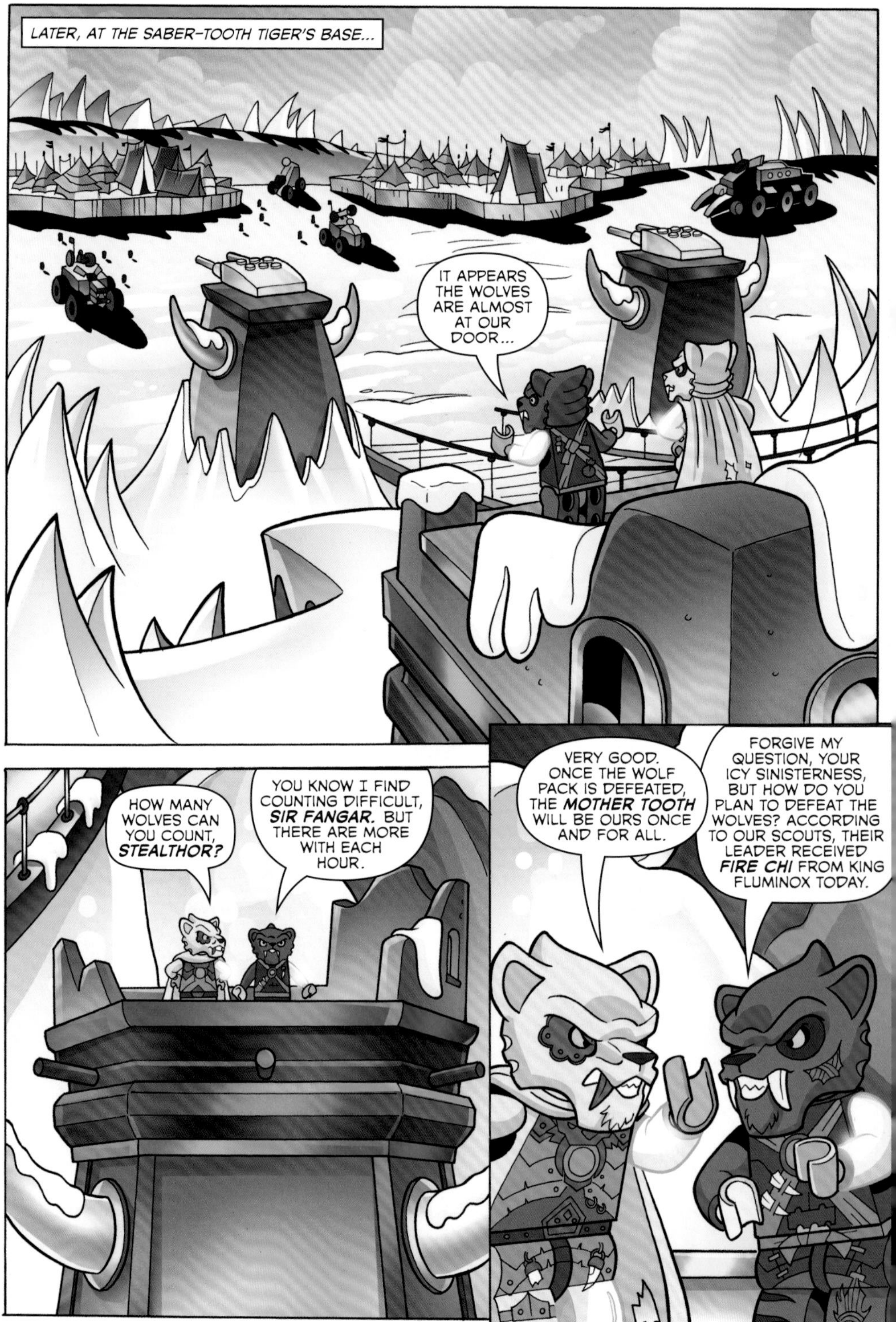
LATER, AT THE SABER-TOOTH TIGER'S BASE...
IT APPEARS THE WOLVES ARE ALMOST AT OUR DOOR...
HOW MANY WOLVES CAN YOU COUNT, **STEALTHOR?**
YOU KNOW I FIND COUNTING DIFFICULT, **SIR FANGAR.** BUT THERE ARE MORE WITH EACH HOUR.
VERY GOOD. ONCE THE WOLF PACK IS DEFEATED, THE ***MOTHER TOOTH*** WILL BE OURS ONCE AND FOR ALL.
FORGIVE MY QUESTION, YOUR ICY SINISTERNESS, BUT HOW DO YOU PLAN TO DEFEAT THE WOLVES? ACCORDING TO OUR SCOUTS, THEIR LEADER RECEIVED ***FIRE CHI*** FROM KING FLUMINOX TODAY.

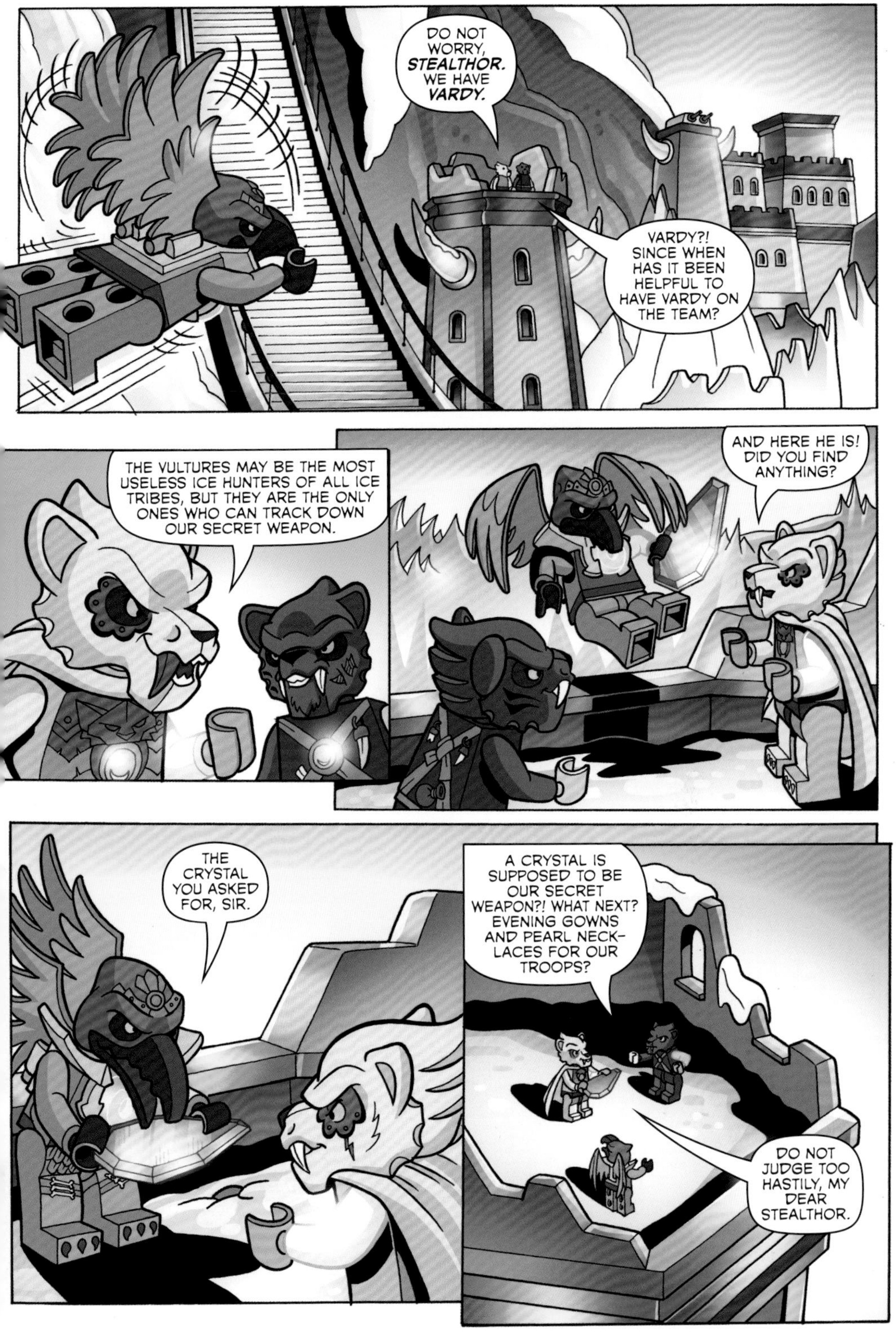
DO NOT WORRY, STEALTHOR. WE HAVE VARDY.
VARDY?! SINCE WHEN HAS IT BEEN HELPFUL TO HAVE VARDY ON THE TEAM?
THE VULTURES MAY BE THE MOST USELESS ICE HUNTERS OF ALL ICE TRIBES, BUT THEY ARE THE ONLY ONES WHO CAN TRACK DOWN OUR SECRET WEAPON.
AND HERE HE IS! DID YOU FIND ANYTHING?
THE CRYSTAL YOU ASKED FOR, SIR.
A CRYSTAL IS SUPPOSED TO BE OUR SECRET WEAPON?! WHAT NEXT? EVENING GOWNS AND PEARL NECK-LACES FOR OUR TROOPS?
DO NOT JUDGE TOO HASTILY, MY DEAR STEALTHOR.

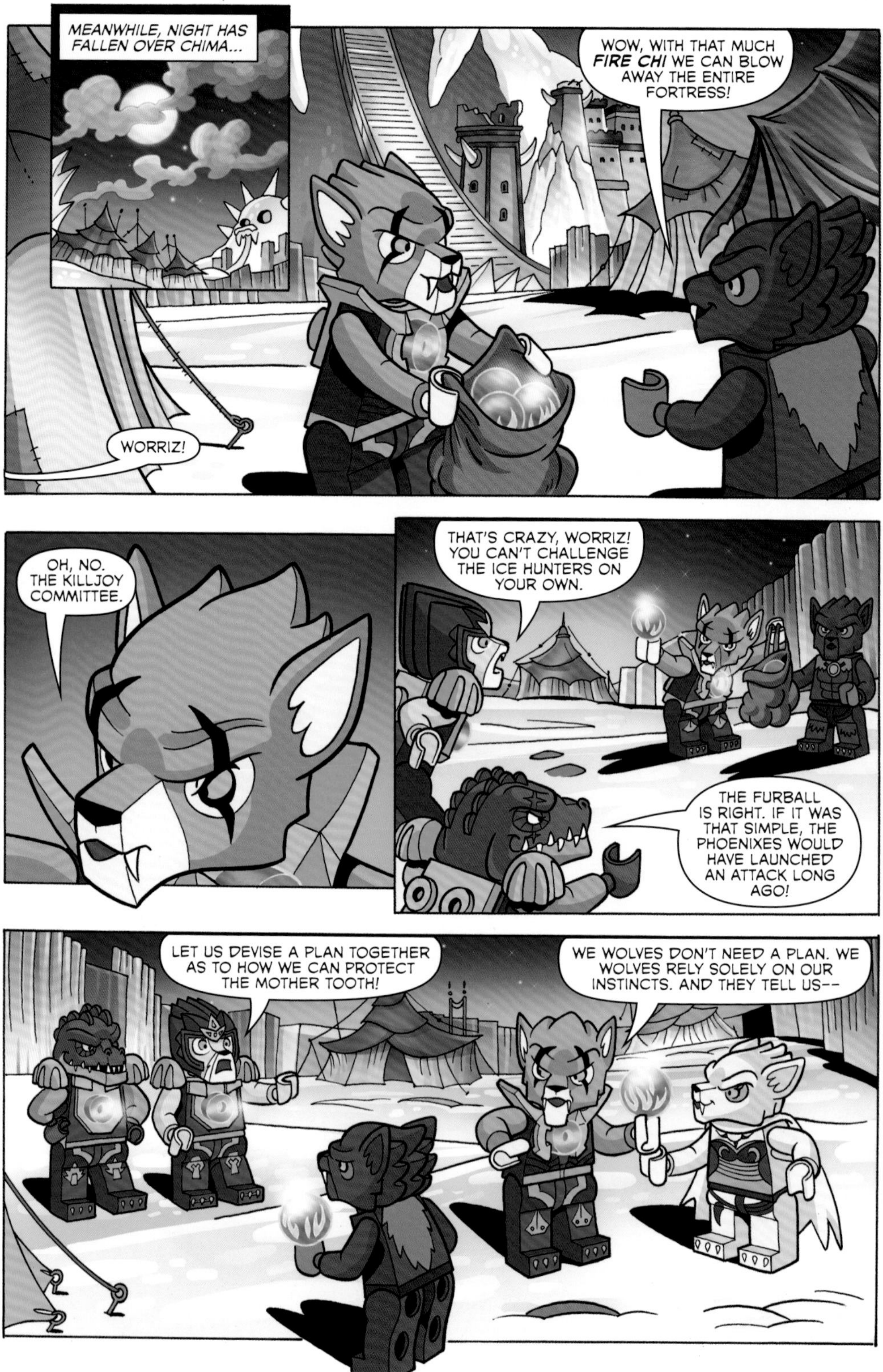
MEANWHILE, NIGHT HAS FALLEN OVER CHIMA...
WOW, WITH THAT MUCH FIRE CHI WE CAN BLOW AWAY THE ENTIRE FORTRESS!
WORRIZ!
OH, NO. THE KILLJOY COMMITTEE.
THAT'S CRAZY, WORRIZ! YOU CAN'T CHALLENGE THE ICE HUNTERS ON YOUR OWN.
THE FURBALL IS RIGHT. IF IT WAS THAT SIMPLE, THE PHOENIXES WOULD HAVE LAUNCHED AN ATTACK LONG AGO!
LET US DEVISE A PLAN TOGETHER AS TO HOW WE CAN PROTECT THE MOTHER TOOTH!
WE WOLVES DON'T NEED A PLAN. WE WOLVES RELY SOLELY ON OUR INSTINCTS. AND THEY TELL US--

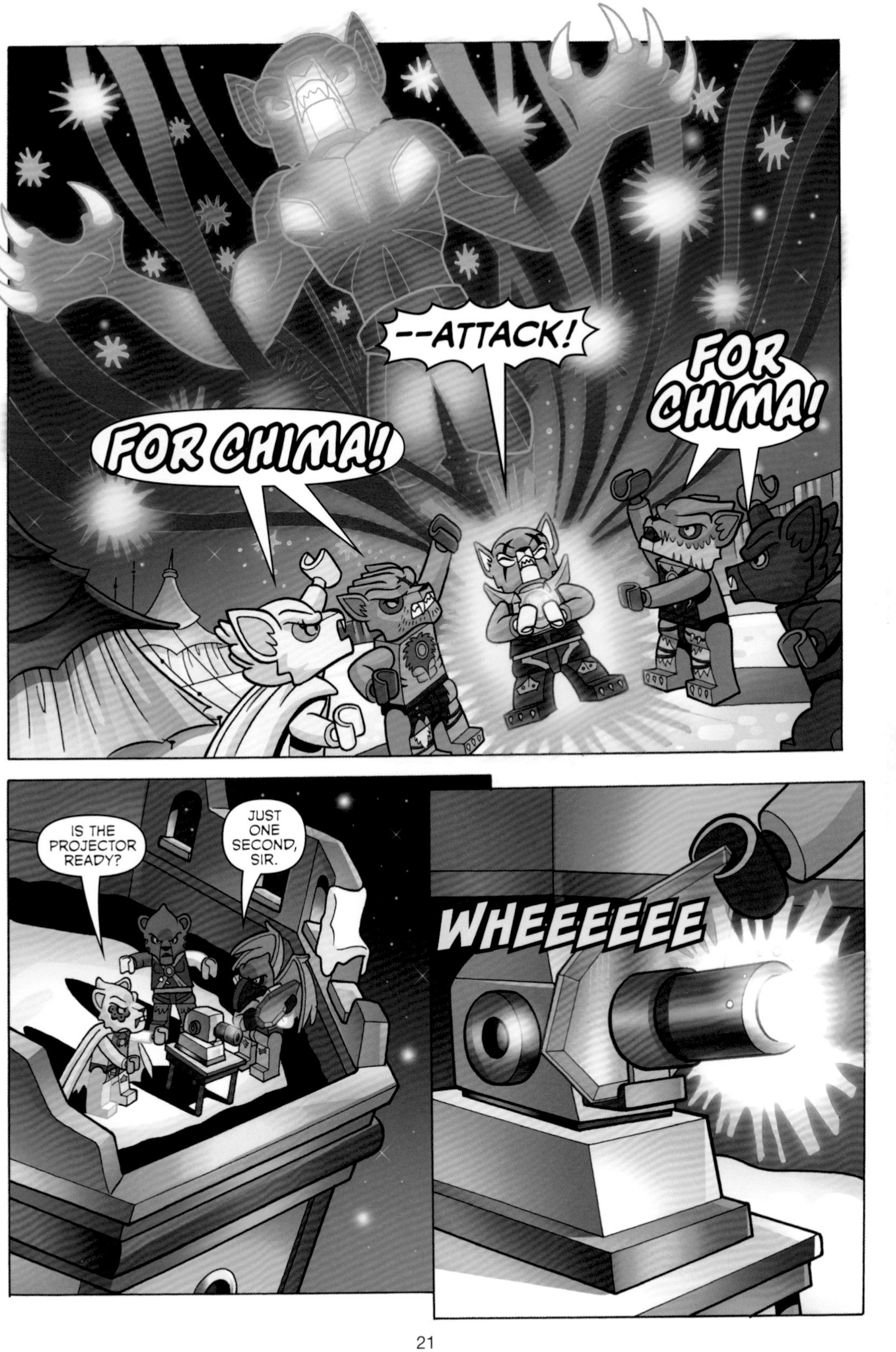
--ATTACK!
FOR CHIMA!
FOR CHIMA!
IS THE PROJECTOR READY?
JUST ONE SECOND, SIR.
WHEEEEEE

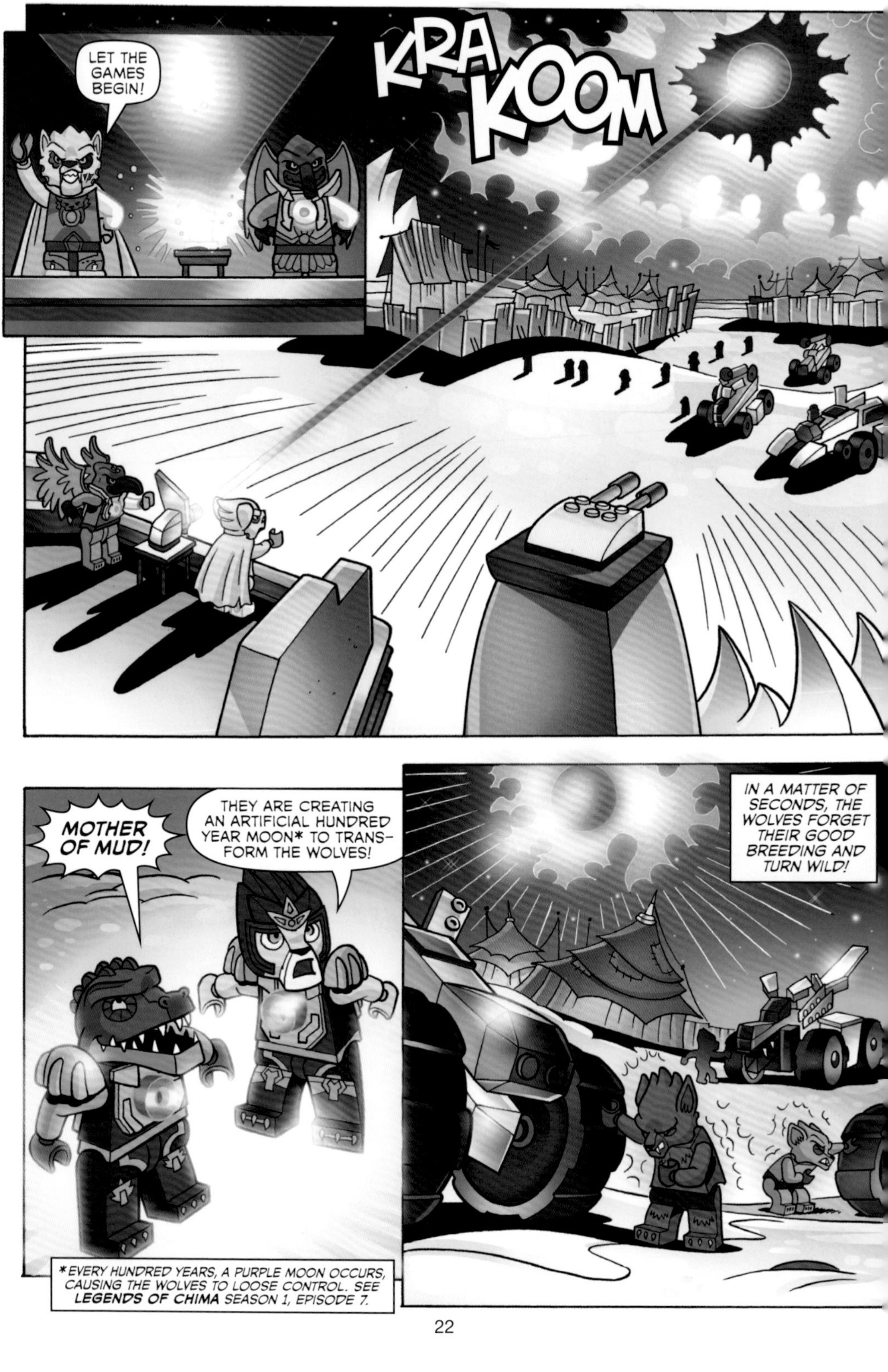
LET THE GAMES BEGIN!
KRA KOOM
MOTHER OF MUD!
THEY ARE CREATING AN ARTIFICIAL HUNDRED YEAR MOON* TO TRANS- FORM THE WOLVES!
*EVERY HUNDRED YEARS, A PURPLE MOON OCCURS, CAUSING THE WOLVES TO LOOSE CONTROL. SEE LEGENDS OF CHIMA SEASON 1, EPISODE 7.
IN A MATTER OF SECONDS, THE WOLVES FORGET THEIR GOOD BREEDING AND TURN WILD!

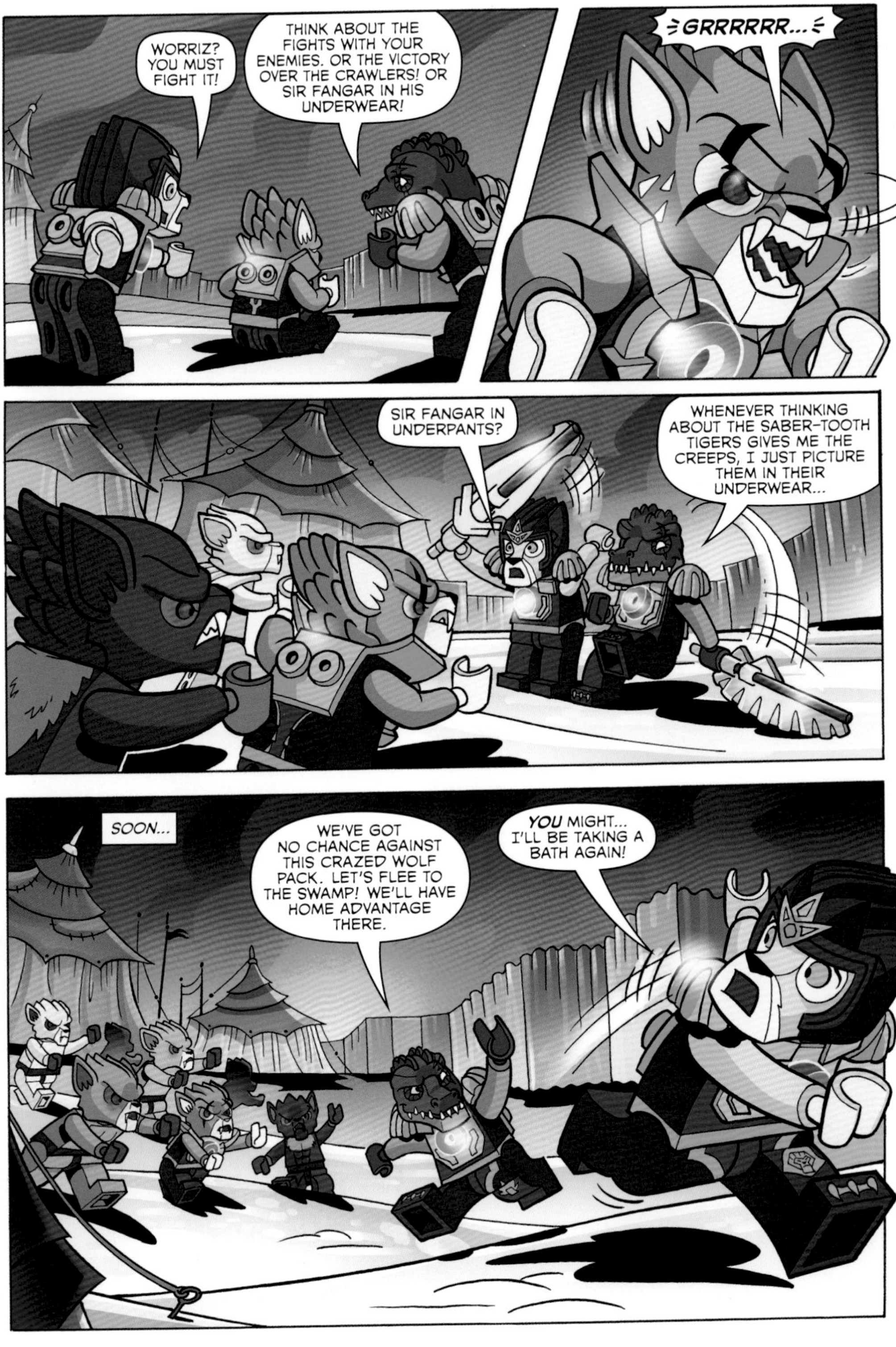
WORRIZ? YOU MUST FIGHT IT!
THINK ABOUT THE FIGHTS WITH YOUR ENEMIES. OR THE VICTORY OVER THE CRAWLERS! OR SIR FANGAR IN HIS UNDERWEAR!
GRRRRRR...
SIR FANGAR IN UNDERPANTS?
WHENEVER THINKING ABOUT THE SABER-TOOTH TIGERS GIVES ME THE CREEPS, I JUST PICTURE THEM IN THEIR UNDERWEAR...
SOON...
WE'VE GOT NO CHANCE AGAINST THIS CRAZED WOLF PACK. LET'S FLEE TO THE SWAMP! WE'LL HAVE HOME ADVANTAGE THERE.
YOU MIGHT... I'LL BE TAKING A BATH AGAIN!

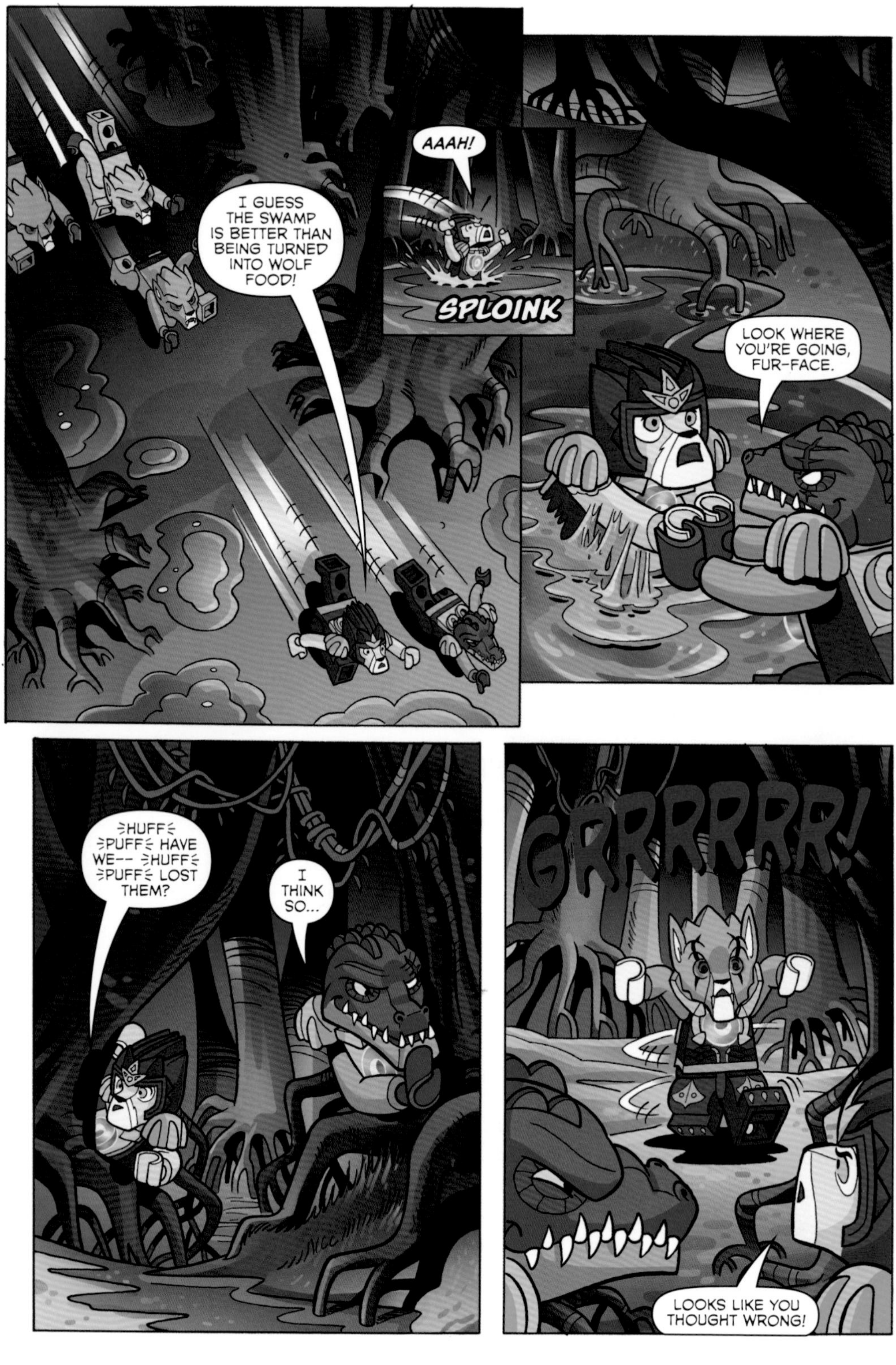
I GUESS THE SWAMP IS BETTER THAN BEING TURNED INTO WOLF FOOD!
AAAH!
SPLOINK
LOOK WHERE YOU'RE GOING, FUR-FACE.
⋛HUFF⋚ ⋛PUFF⋚ HAVE WE-- ⋛HUFF⋚ ⋛PUFF⋚ LOST THEM?
I THINK SO...
GRRRRRR!
LOOKS LIKE YOU THOUGHT WRONG!

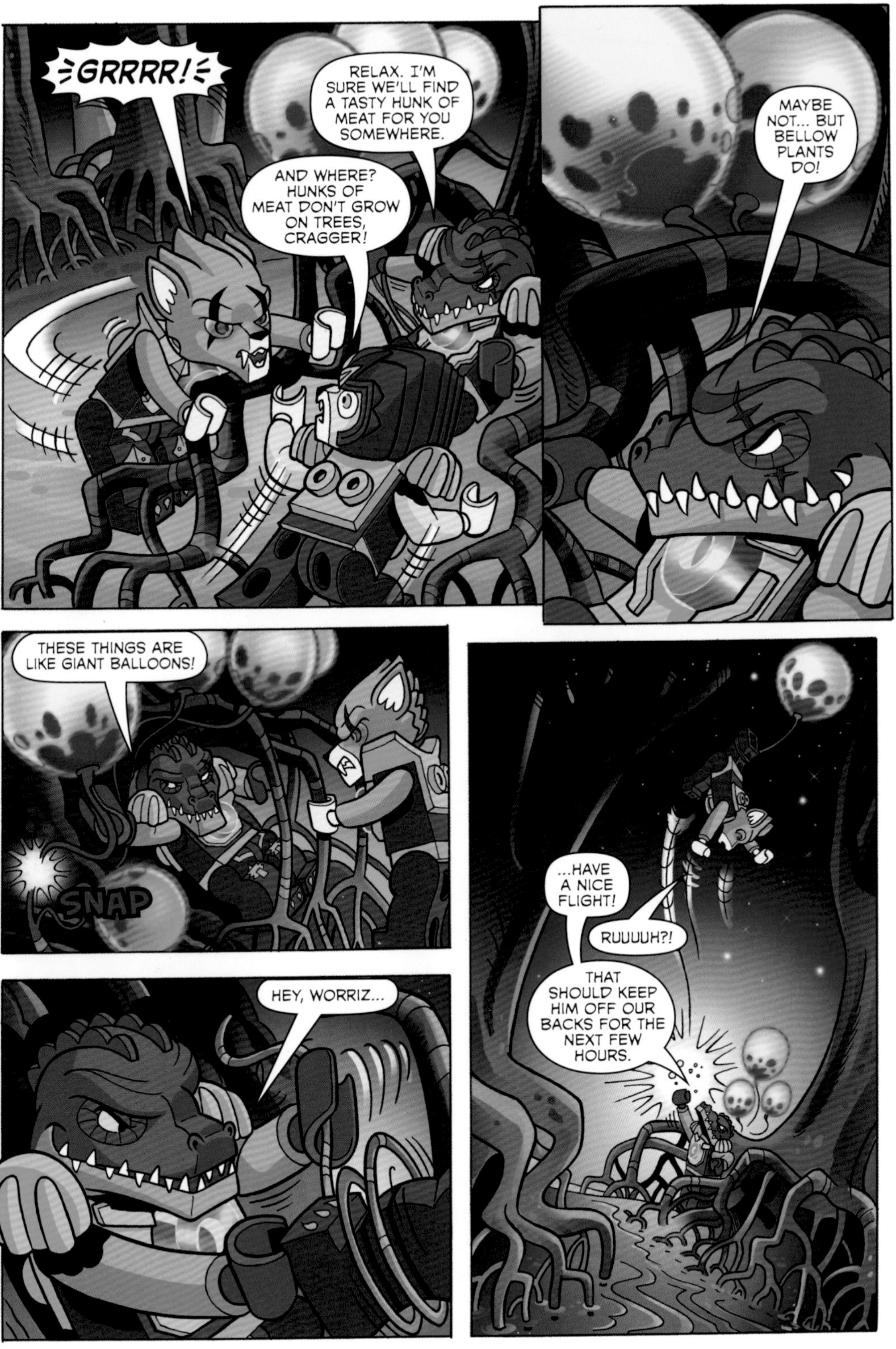
GRRRR!
RELAX. I'M SURE WE'LL FIND A TASTY HUNK OF MEAT FOR YOU SOMEWHERE.
AND WHERE? HUNKS OF MEAT DON'T GROW ON TREES, CRAGGER!
MAYBE NOT... BUT BELLOW PLANTS DO!
THESE THINGS ARE LIKE GIANT BALLOONS!
SNAP
HEY, WORRIZ...
...HAVE A NICE FLIGHT!
RUUUUH?!
THAT SHOULD KEEP HIM OFF OUR BACKS FOR THE NEXT FEW HOURS.

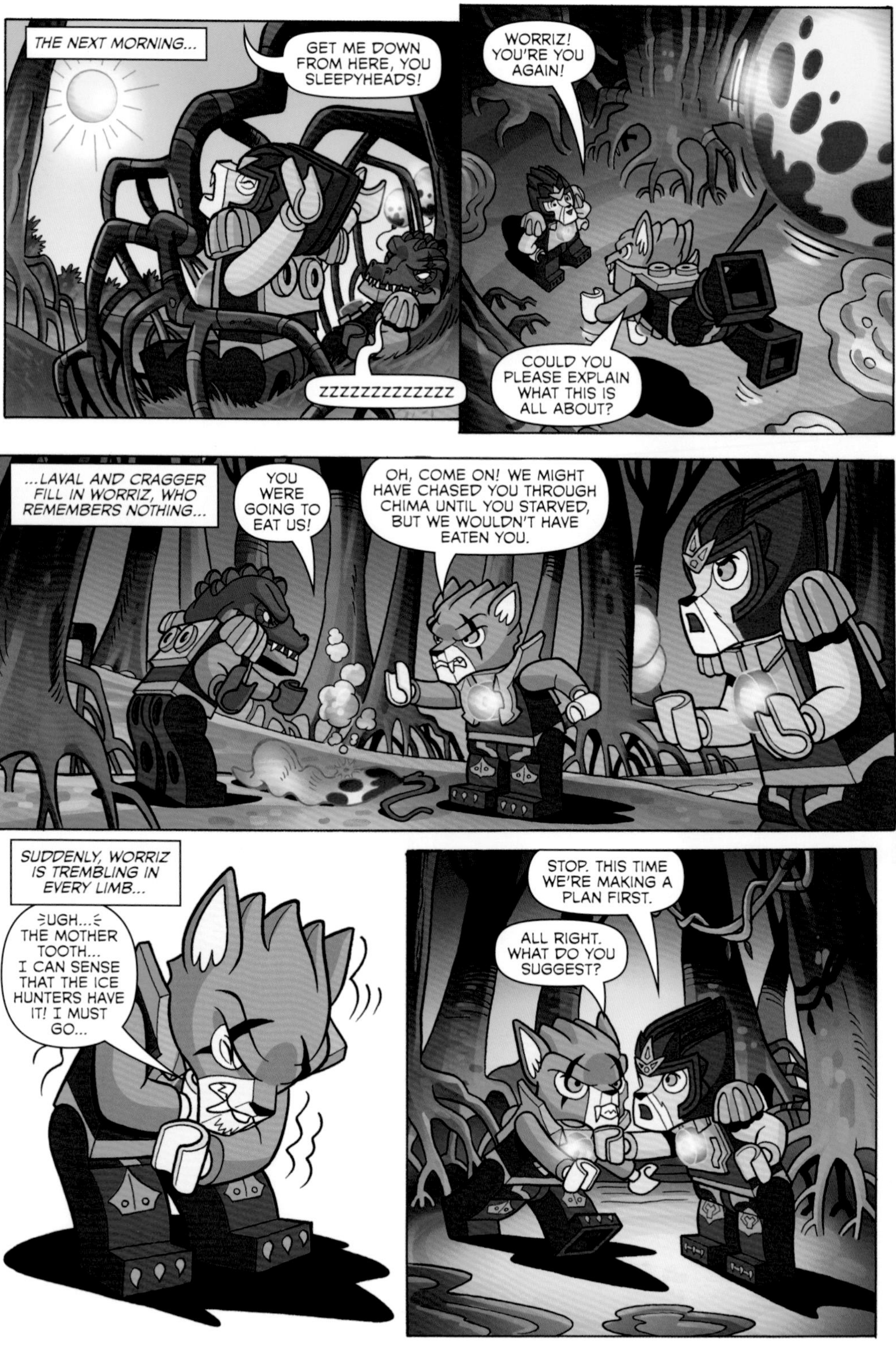

THE NEXT MORNING...
GET ME DOWN FROM HERE, YOU SLEEPYHEADS!
ZZZZZZZZZZZZZ
WORRIZ! YOU'RE YOU AGAIN!
COULD YOU PLEASE EXPLAIN WHAT THIS IS ALL ABOUT?
...LAVAL AND CRAGGER FILL IN WORRIZ, WHO REMEMBERS NOTHING...
YOU WERE GOING TO EAT US!
OH, COME ON! WE MIGHT HAVE CHASED YOU THROUGH CHIMA UNTIL YOU STARVED, BUT WE WOULDN'T HAVE EATEN YOU.
SUDDENLY, WORRIZ IS TREMBLING IN EVERY LIMB...
UGH... THE MOTHER TOOTH... I CAN SENSE THAT THE ICE HUNTERS HAVE IT! I MUST GO...
STOP. THIS TIME WE'RE MAKING A PLAN FIRST.
ALL RIGHT. WHAT DO YOU SUGGEST?

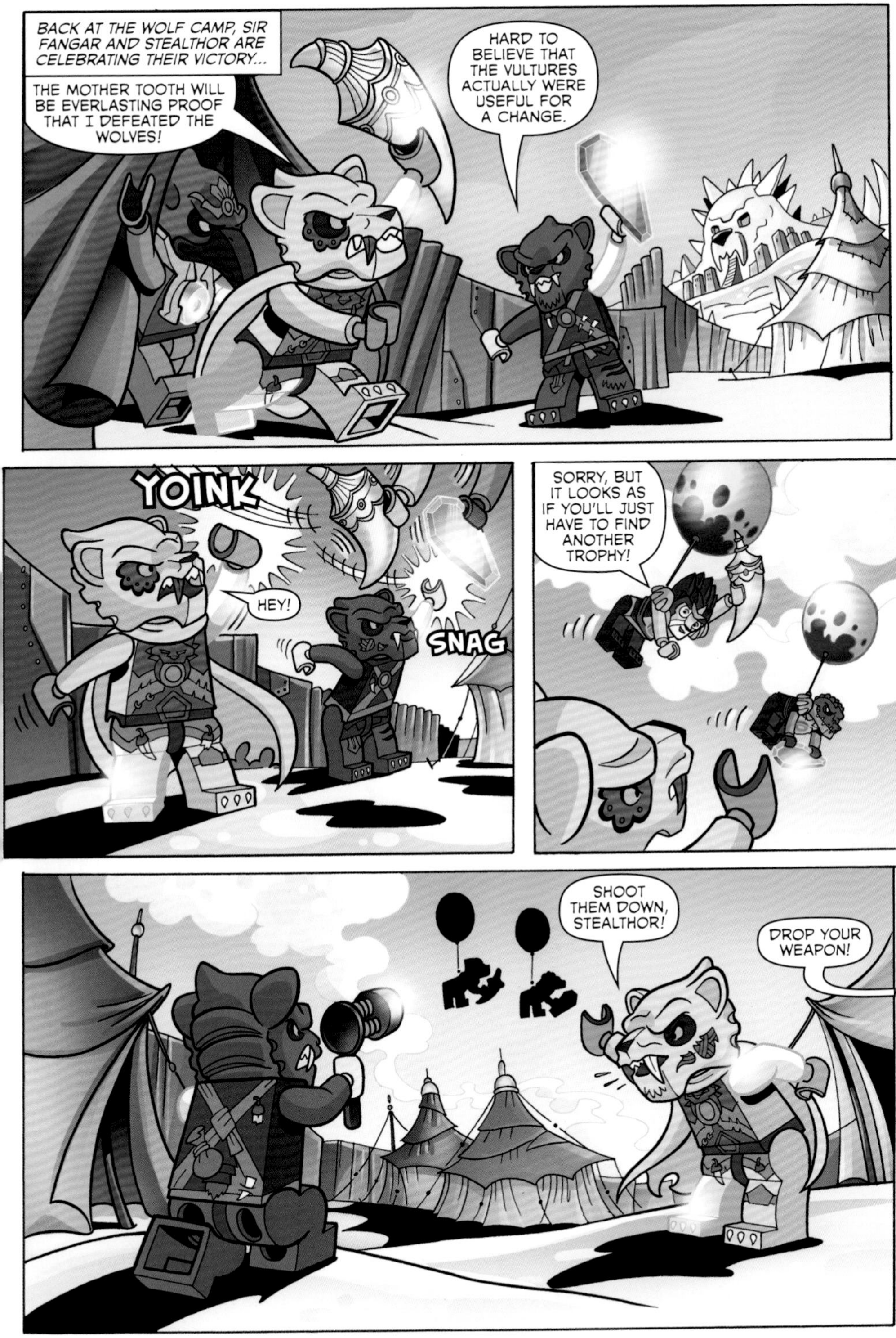
BACK AT THE WOLF CAMP, SIR FANGAR AND STEALTHOR ARE CELEBRATING THEIR VICTORY...
THE MOTHER TOOTH WILL BE EVERLASTING PROOF THAT I DEFEATED THE WOLVES!
HARD TO BELIEVE THAT THE VULTURES ACTUALLY WERE USEFUL FOR A CHANGE.
YOINK
HEY!
SNAG
SORRY, BUT IT LOOKS AS IF YOU'LL JUST HAVE TO FIND ANOTHER TROPHY!
SHOOT THEM DOWN, STEALTHOR!
DROP YOUR WEAPON!

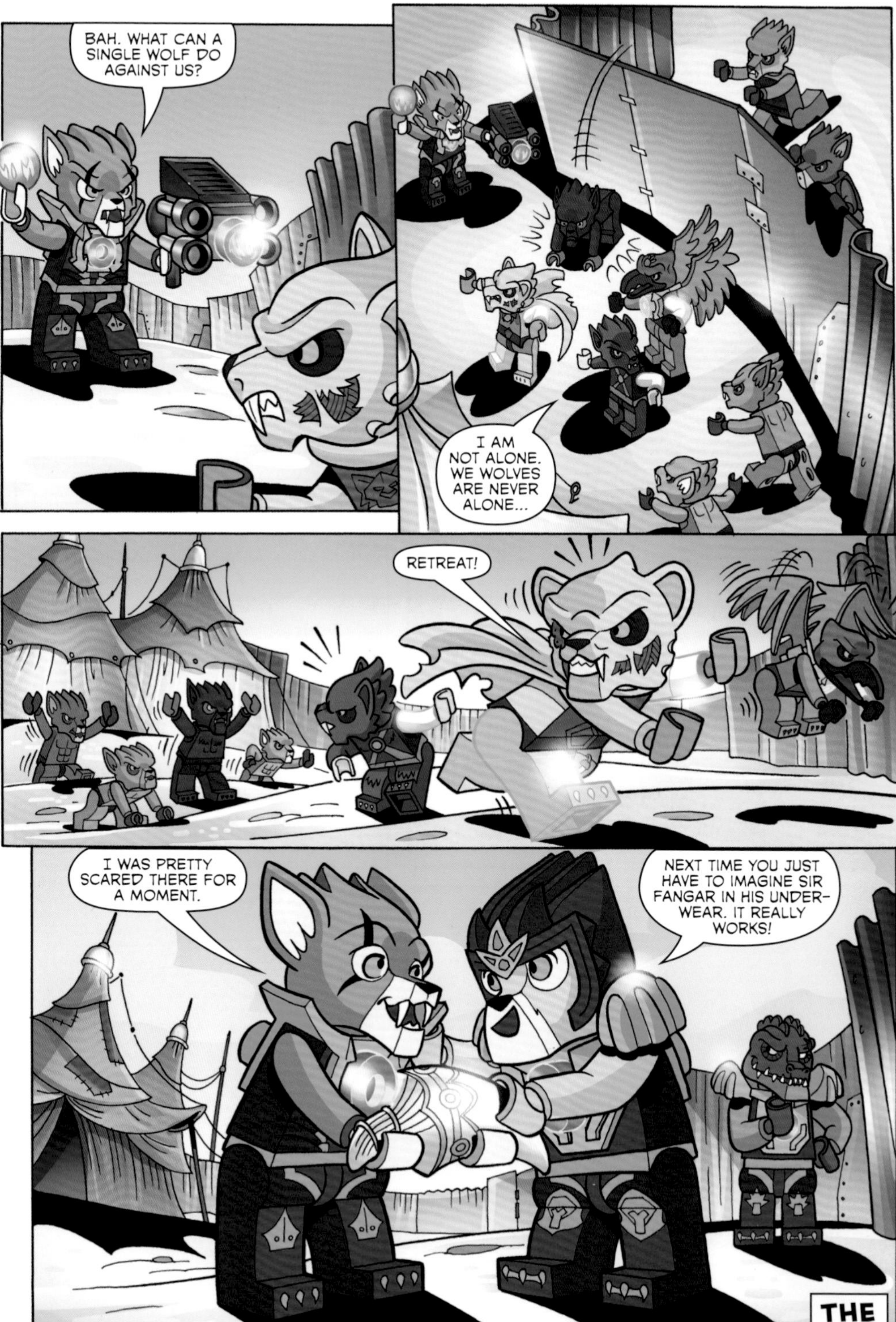
BAH. WHAT CAN A SINGLE WOLF DO AGAINST US?
I AM NOT ALONE. WE WOLVES ARE NEVER ALONE...
RETREAT!
I WAS PRETTY SCARED THERE FOR A MOMENT.
NEXT TIME YOU JUST HAVE TO IMAGINE SIR FANGAR IN HIS UNDER-WEAR. IT REALLY WORKS!
THE END

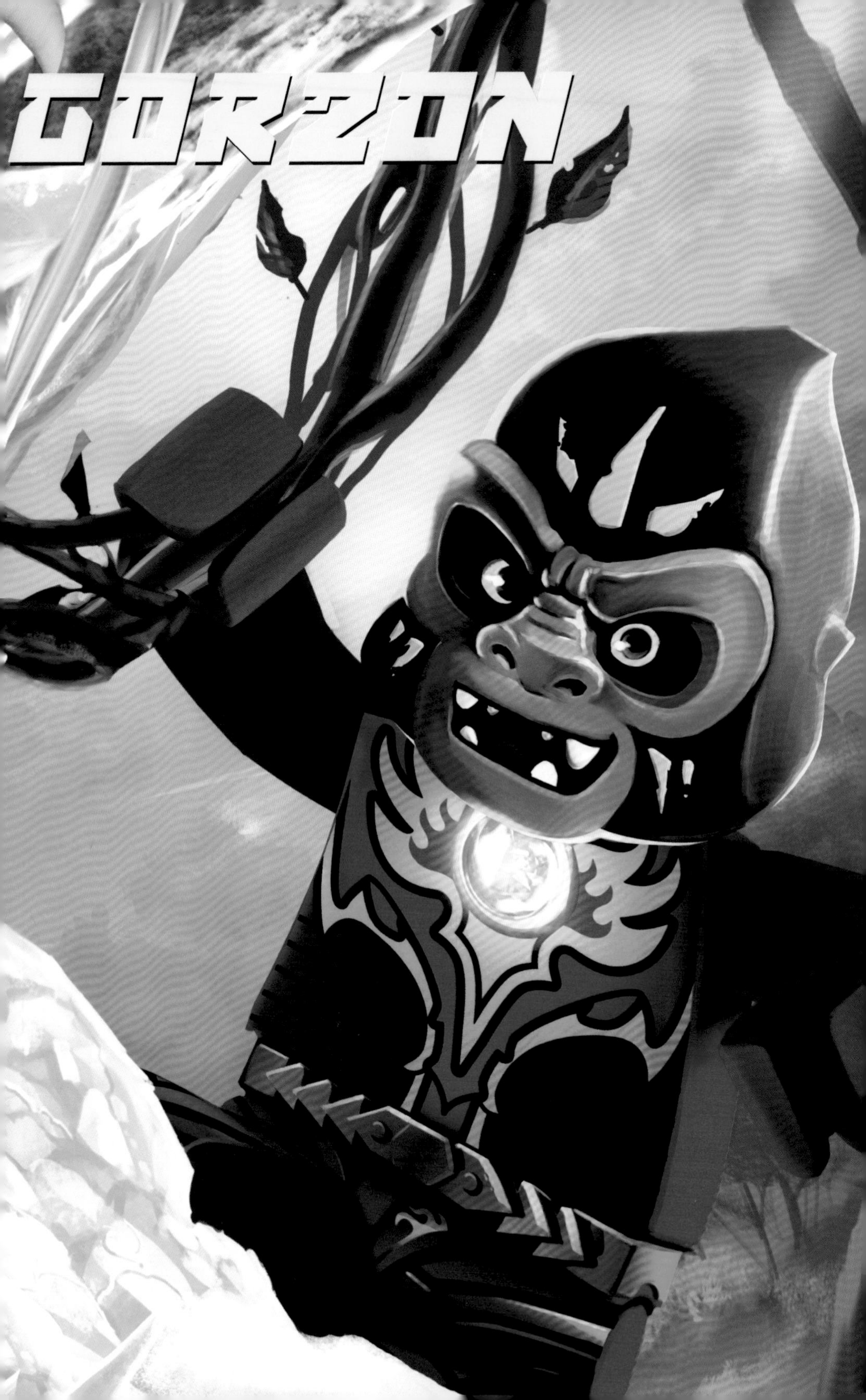
GORZON

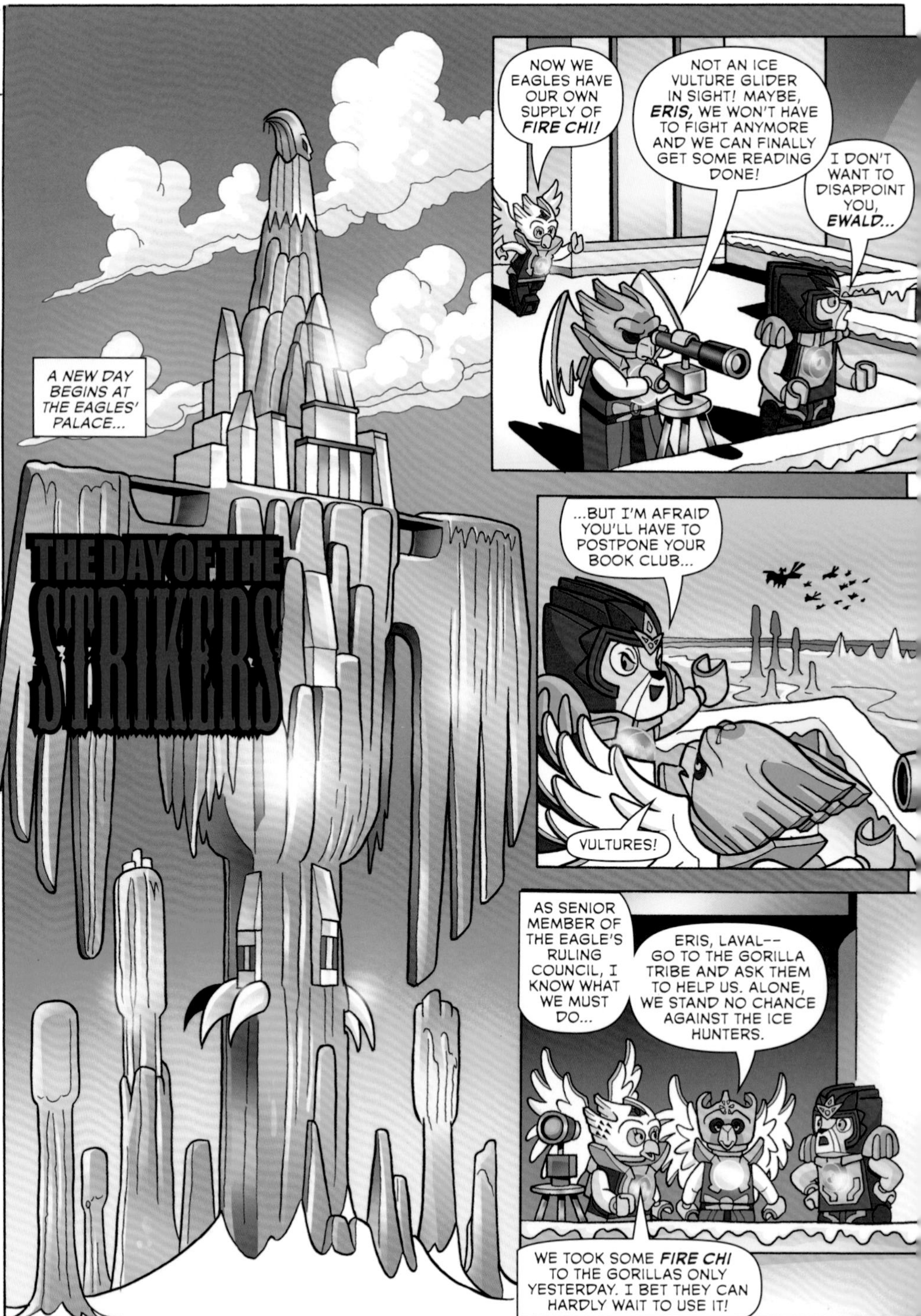

A NEW DAY BEGINS AT THE EAGLES' PALACE...
THE DAY OF THE STRIKERS
NOW WE EAGLES HAVE OUR OWN SUPPLY OF FIRE CHI!
NOT AN ICE VULTURE GLIDER IN SIGHT! MAYBE, ERIS, WE WON'T HAVE TO FIGHT ANYMORE AND WE CAN FINALLY GET SOME READING DONE!
I DON'T WANT TO DISAPPOINT YOU, EWALD...
...BUT I'M AFRAID YOU'LL HAVE TO POSTPONE YOUR BOOK CLUB...
VULTURES!
AS SENIOR MEMBER OF THE EAGLE'S RULING COUNCIL, I KNOW WHAT WE MUST DO...
ERIS, LAVAL-- GO TO THE GORILLA TRIBE AND ASK THEM TO HELP US. ALONE, WE STAND NO CHANCE AGAINST THE ICE HUNTERS.
WE TOOK SOME FIRE CHI TO THE GORILLAS ONLY YESTERDAY. I BET THEY CAN HARDLY WAIT TO USE IT!

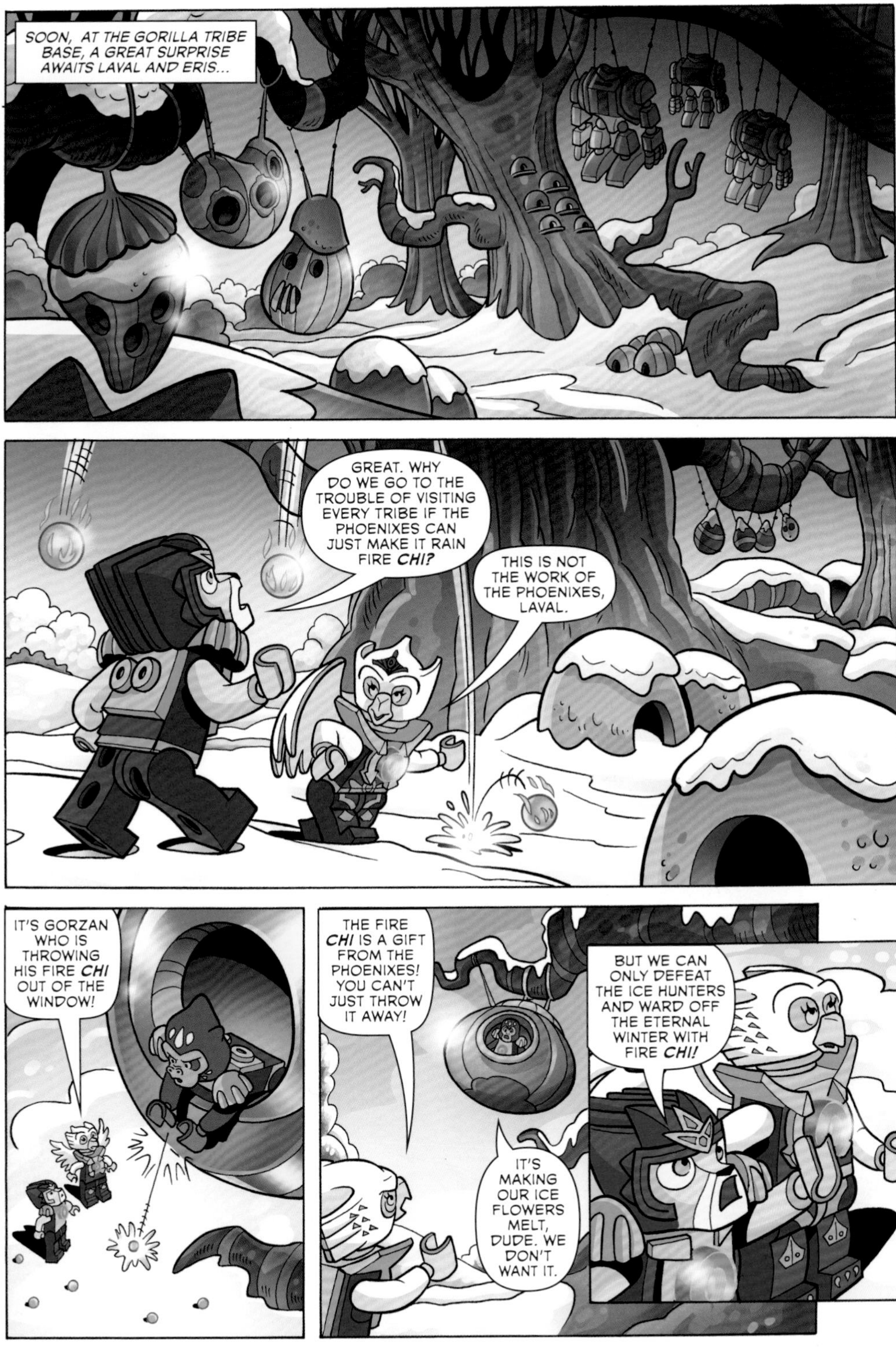
SOON, AT THE GORILLA TRIBE BASE, A GREAT SURPRISE AWAITS LAVAL AND ERIS...
GREAT. WHY DO WE GO TO THE TROUBLE OF VISITING EVERY TRIBE IF THE PHOENIXES CAN JUST MAKE IT RAIN FIRE CHI?
THIS IS NOT THE WORK OF THE PHOENIXES, LAVAL.
IT'S GORZAN WHO IS THROWING HIS FIRE CHI OUT OF THE WINDOW!
THE FIRE CHI IS A GIFT FROM THE PHOENIXES! YOU CAN'T JUST THROW IT AWAY!
IT'S MAKING OUR ICE FLOWERS MELT, DUDE. WE DON'T WANT IT.
BUT WE CAN ONLY DEFEAT THE ICE HUNTERS AND WARD OFF THE ETERNAL WINTER WITH FIRE CHI!

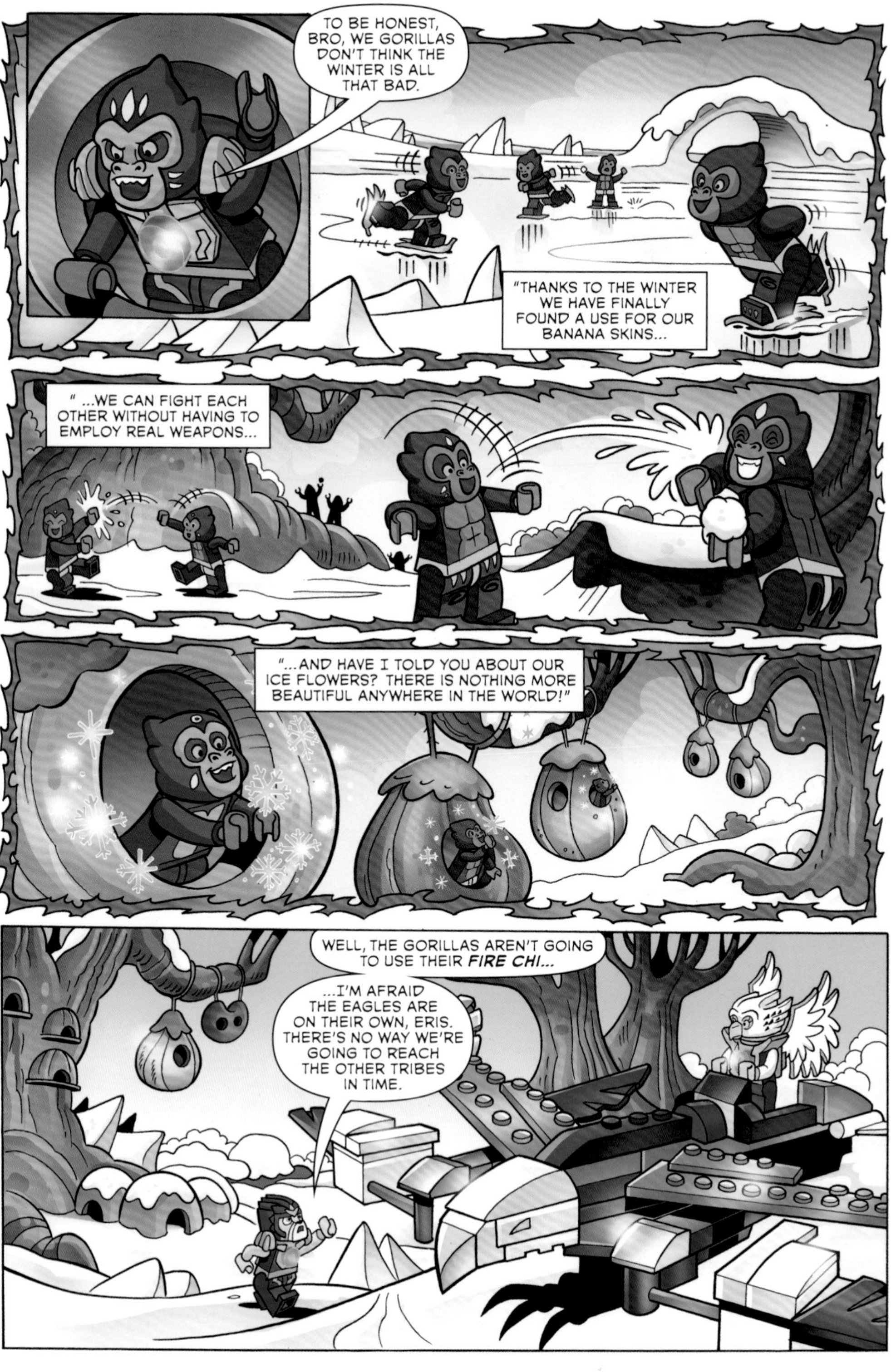
TO BE HONEST, BRO, WE GORILLAS DON'T THINK THE WINTER IS ALL THAT BAD.
"THANKS TO THE WINTER WE HAVE FINALLY FOUND A USE FOR OUR BANANA SKINS...
" ...WE CAN FIGHT EACH OTHER WITHOUT HAVING TO EMPLOY REAL WEAPONS...
"...AND HAVE I TOLD YOU ABOUT OUR ICE FLOWERS? THERE IS NOTHING MORE BEAUTIFUL ANYWHERE IN THE WORLD!"
WELL, THE GORILLAS AREN'T GOING TO USE THEIR *FIRE CHI...*
...I'M AFRAID THE EAGLES ARE ON THEIR OWN, ERIS. THERE'S NO WAY WE'RE GOING TO REACH THE OTHER TRIBES IN TIME.

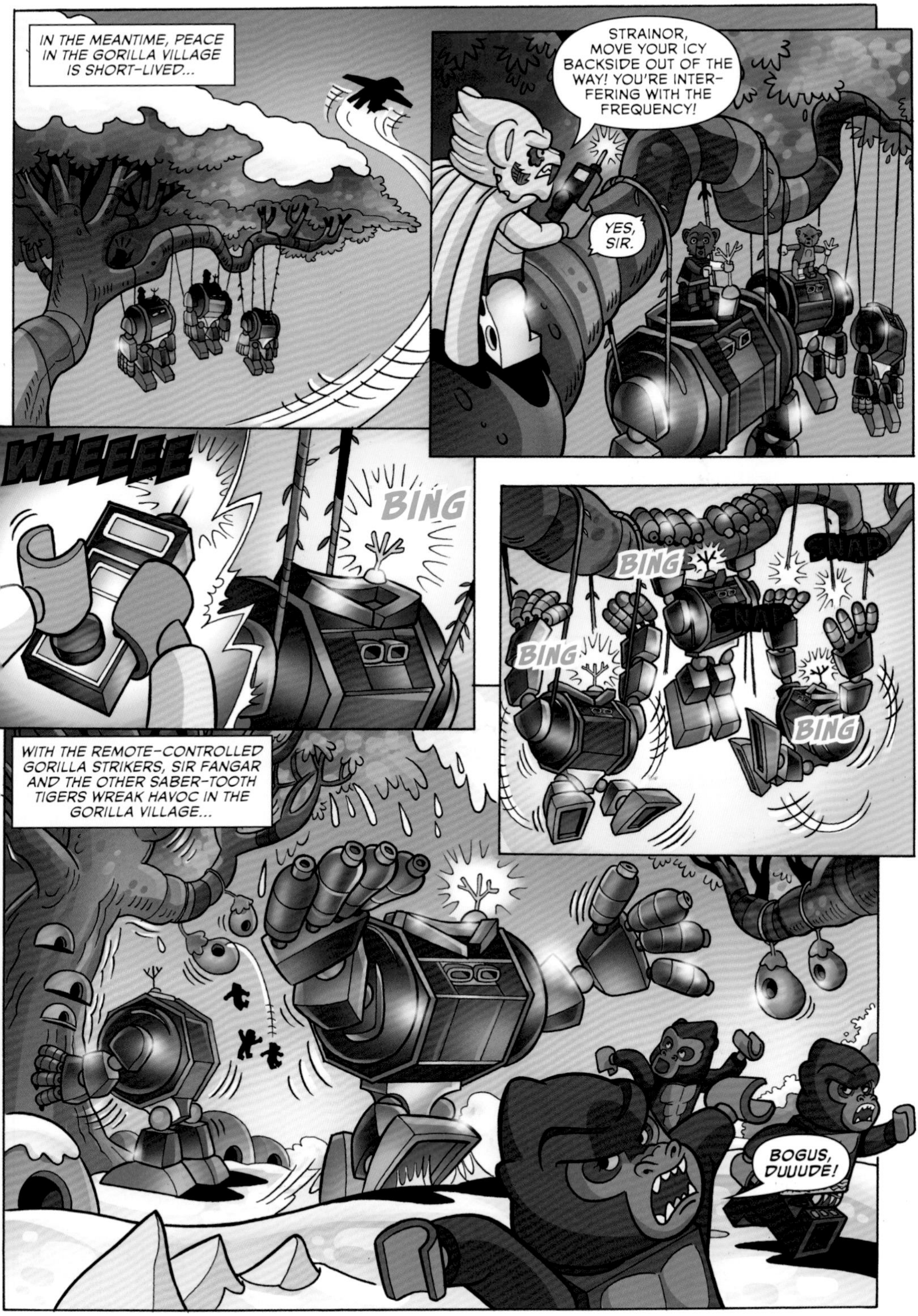
IN THE MEANTIME, PEACE IN THE GORILLA VILLAGE IS SHORT-LIVED...
STRAINOR, MOVE YOUR ICY BACKSIDE OUT OF THE WAY! YOU'RE INTER-FERING WITH THE FREQUENCY!
YES, SIR.
WHEEEE
BING
BING
SNAP
BING
SNAP
BING
WITH THE REMOTE-CONTROLLED GORILLA STRIKERS, SIR FANGAR AND THE OTHER SABER-TOOTH TIGERS WREAK HAVOC IN THE GORILLA VILLAGE...
BOGUS, DUUUDE!

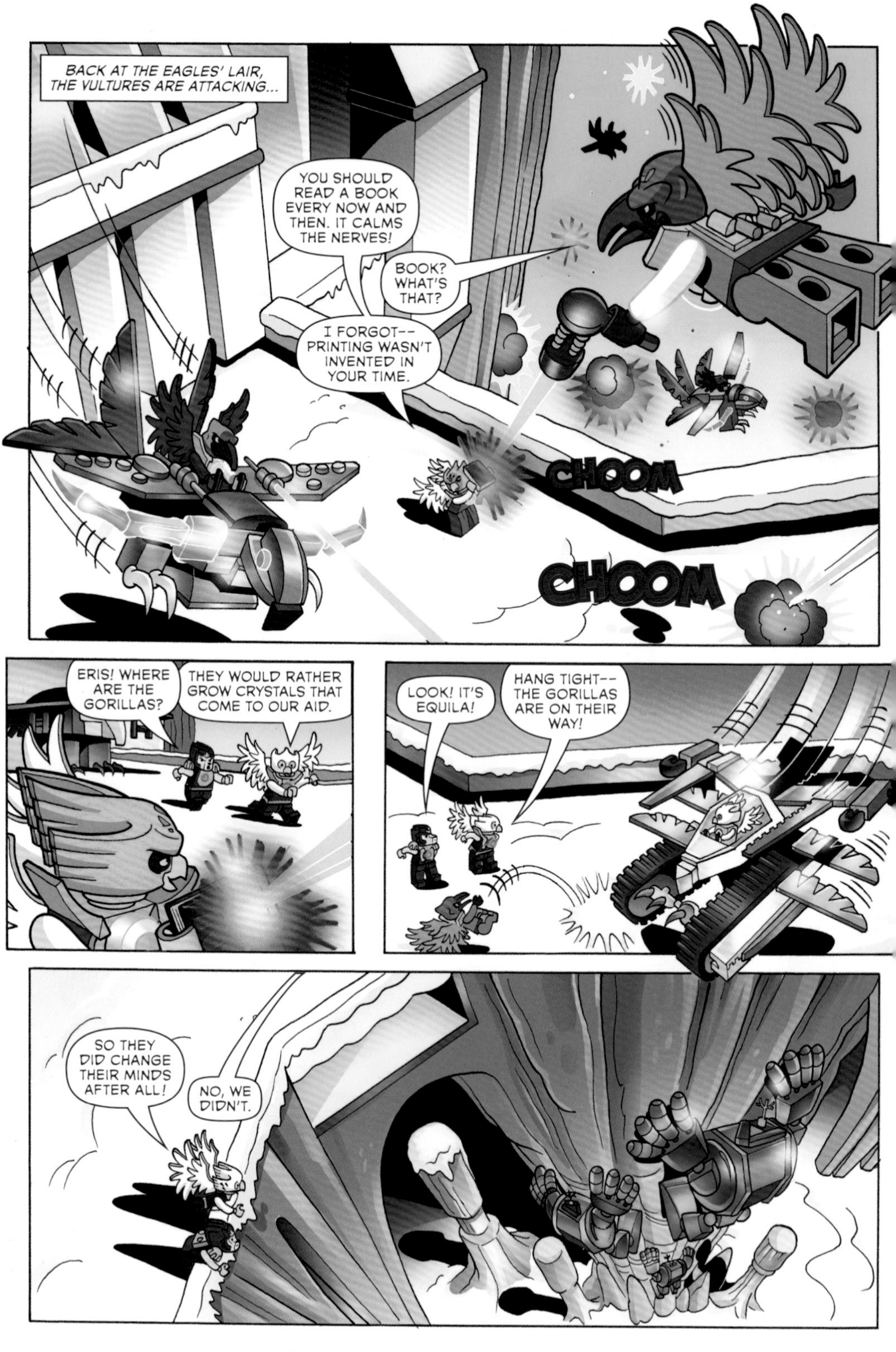
BACK AT THE EAGLES' LAIR, THE VULTURES ARE ATTACKING...
YOU SHOULD READ A BOOK EVERY NOW AND THEN. IT CALMS THE NERVES!
BOOK? WHAT'S THAT?
I FORGOT-- PRINTING WASN'T INVENTED IN YOUR TIME.
CHOOM
CHOOM
ERIS! WHERE ARE THE GORILLAS?
THEY WOULD RATHER GROW CRYSTALS THAT COME TO OUR AID.
LOOK! IT'S EQUILA!
HANG TIGHT-- THE GORILLAS ARE ON THEIR WAY!
SO THEY DID CHANGE THEIR MINDS AFTER ALL!
NO, WE DIDN'T.

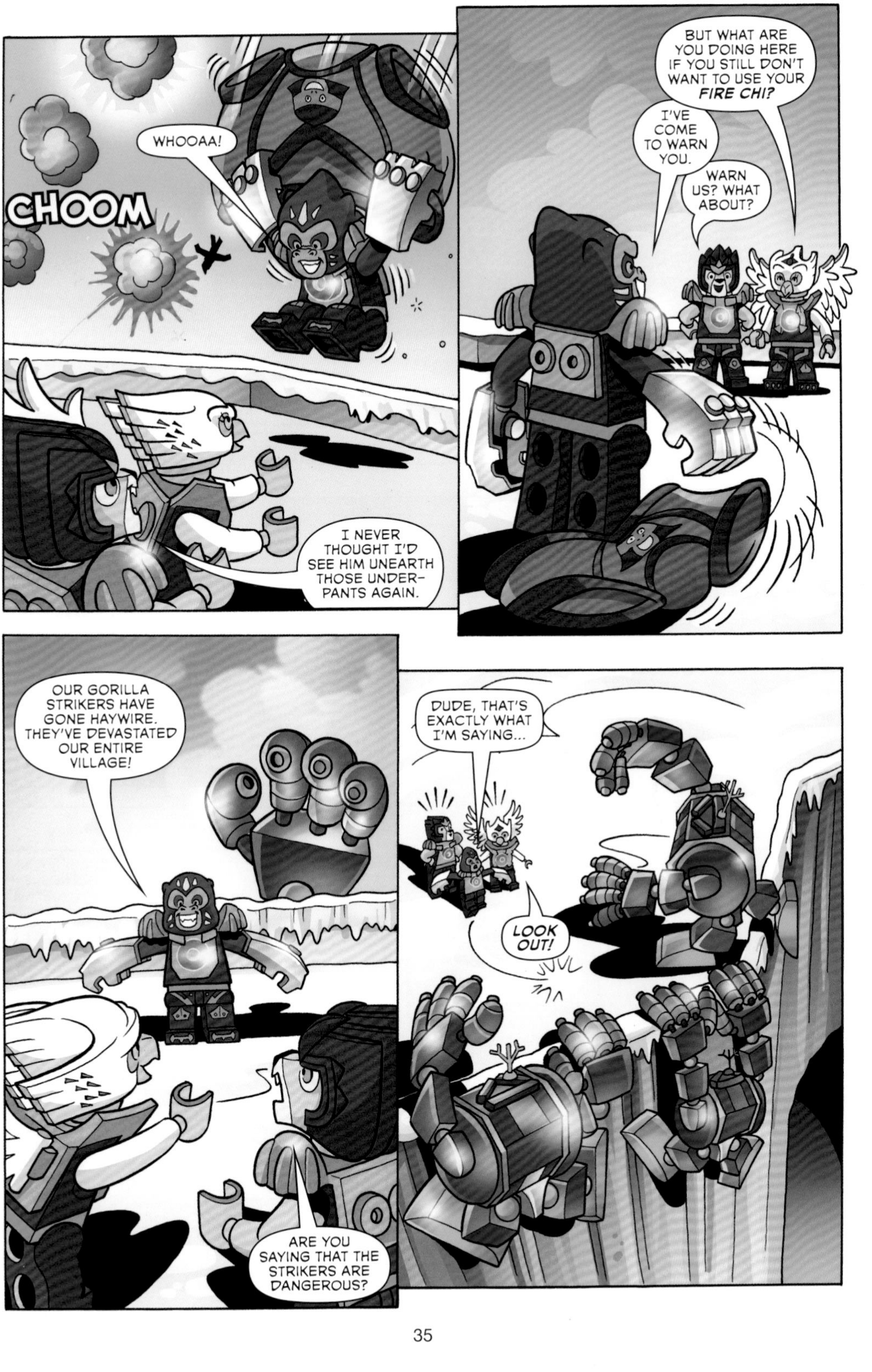

WHOOAA!
CHOOM
I NEVER THOUGHT I'D SEE HIM UNEARTH THOSE UNDER-PANTS AGAIN.
BUT WHAT ARE YOU DOING HERE IF YOU STILL DON'T WANT TO USE YOUR *FIRE CHI?*
I'VE COME TO WARN YOU.
WARN US? WHAT ABOUT?
OUR GORILLA STRIKERS HAVE GONE HAYWIRE. THEY'VE DEVASTATED OUR ENTIRE VILLAGE!
ARE YOU SAYING THAT THE STRIKERS ARE DANGEROUS?
DUDE, THAT'S EXACTLY WHAT I'M SAYING...
LOOK OUT!

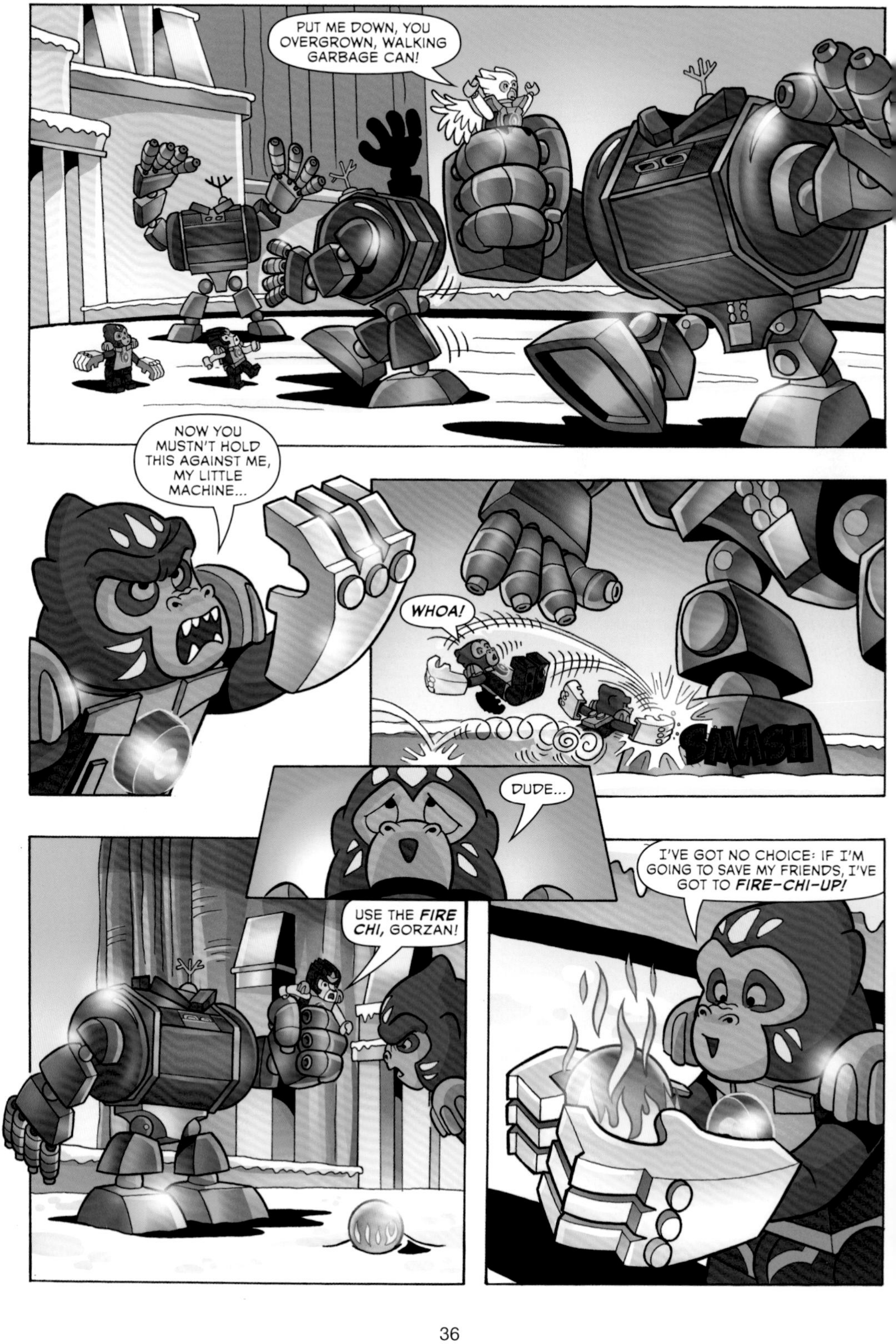
PUT ME DOWN, YOU OVERGROWN, WALKING GARBAGE CAN!
NOW YOU MUSTN'T HOLD THIS AGAINST ME, MY LITTLE MACHINE...
WHOA!
SMASH
DUDE...
USE THE FIRE CHI, GORZAN!
I'VE GOT NO CHOICE: IF I'M GOING TO SAVE MY FRIENDS, I'VE GOT TO FIRE-CHI-UP!

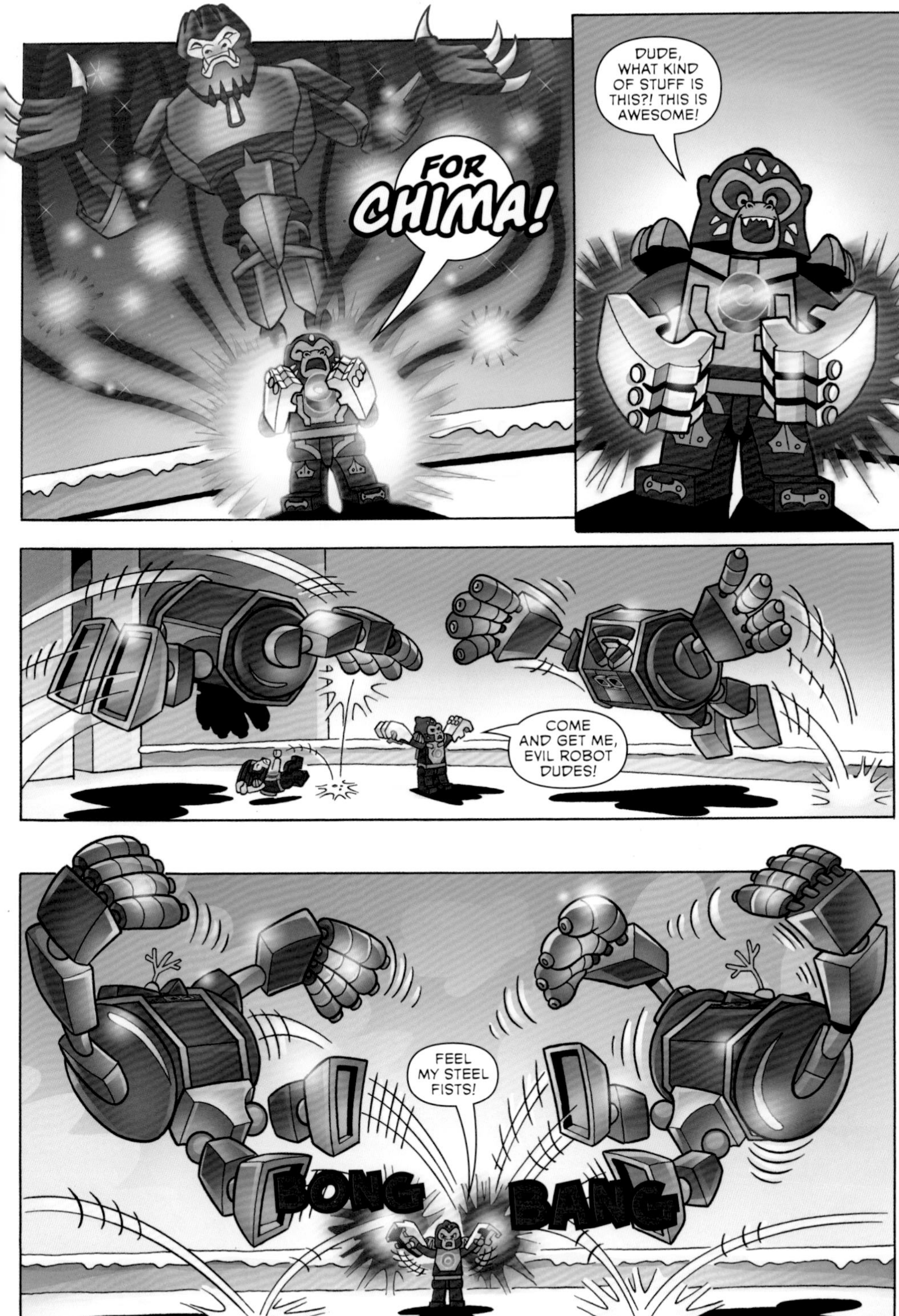
FOR CHIMA!
DUDE, WHAT KIND OF STUFF IS THIS?! THIS IS AWESOME!
COME AND GET ME, EVIL ROBOT DUDES!
FEEL MY STEEL FISTS!
BONG
BANG

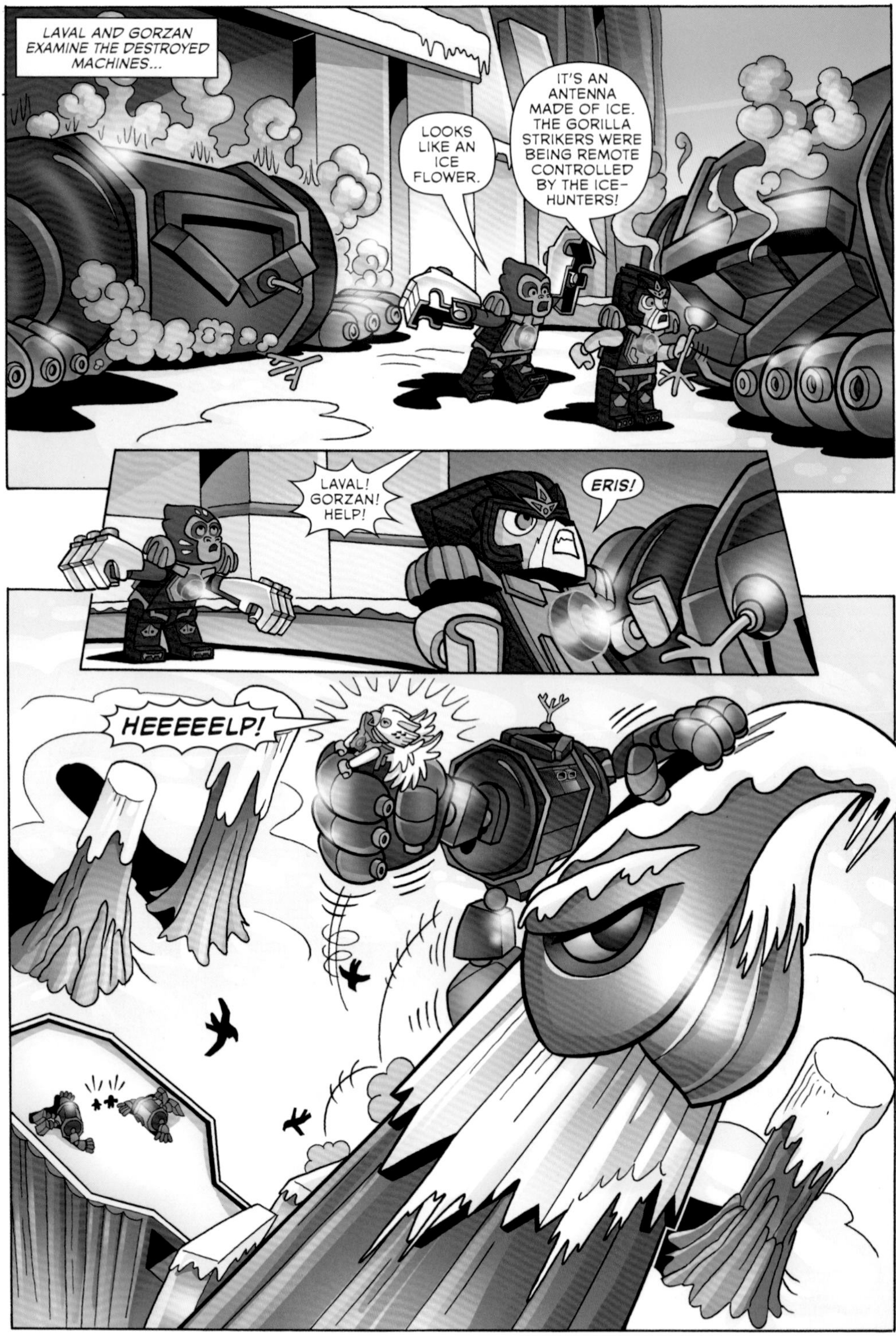
LAVAL AND GORZAN EXAMINE THE DESTROYED MACHINES...
LOOKS LIKE AN ICE FLOWER.
IT'S AN ANTENNA MADE OF ICE. THE GORILLA STRIKERS WERE BEING REMOTE CONTROLLED BY THE ICE-HUNTERS!
LAVAL! GORZAN! HELP!
ERIS!
HEEEEELP!

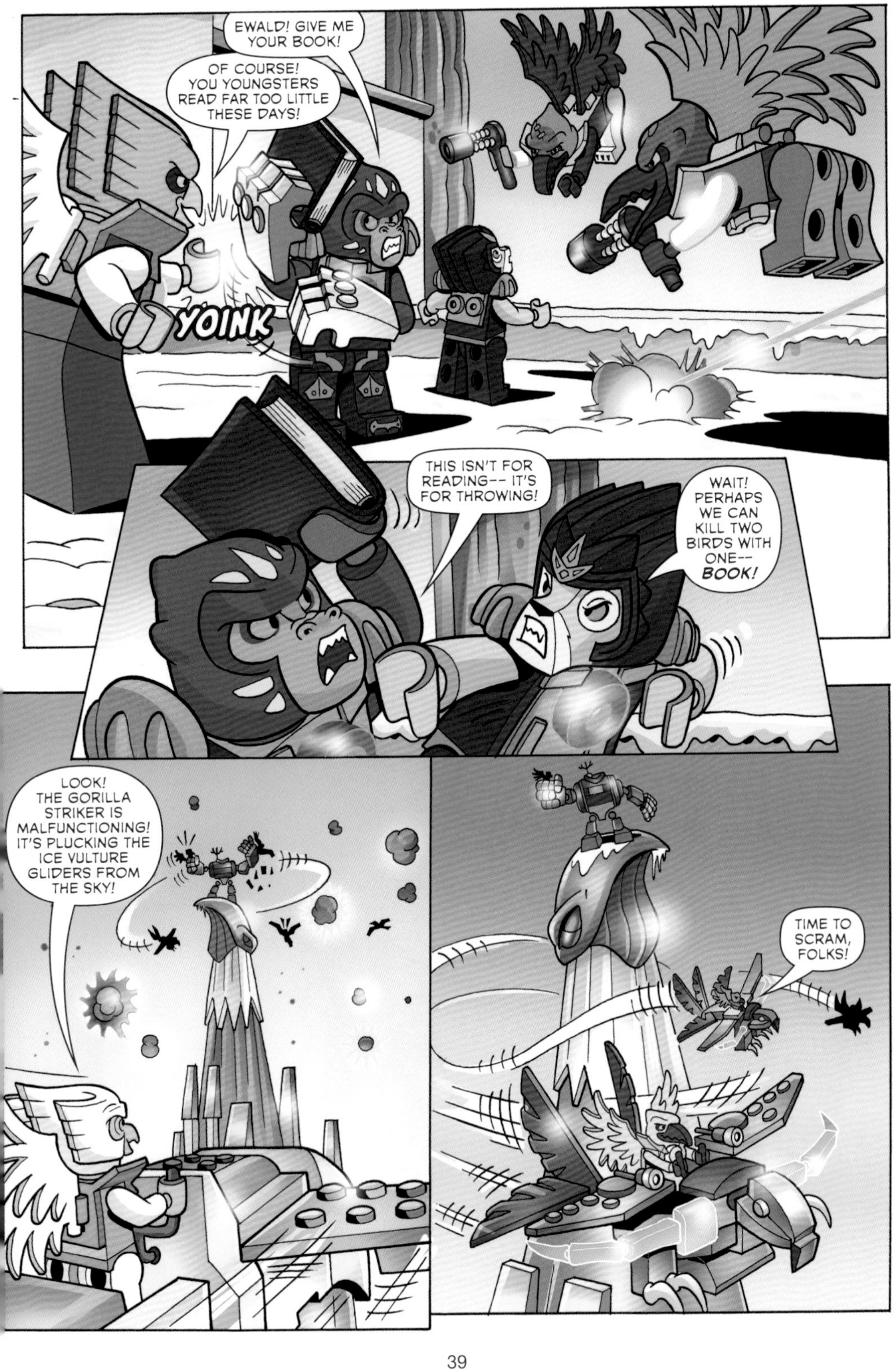
EWALD! GIVE ME YOUR BOOK!
OF COURSE! YOU YOUNGSTERS READ FAR TOO LITTLE THESE DAYS!
YOINK
THIS ISN'T FOR READING-- IT'S FOR THROWING!
WAIT! PERHAPS WE CAN KILL TWO BIRDS WITH ONE-- BOOK!
LOOK! THE GORILLA STRIKER IS MALFUNCTIONING! IT'S PLUCKING THE ICE VULTURE GLIDERS FROM THE SKY!
TIME TO SCRAM, FOLKS!

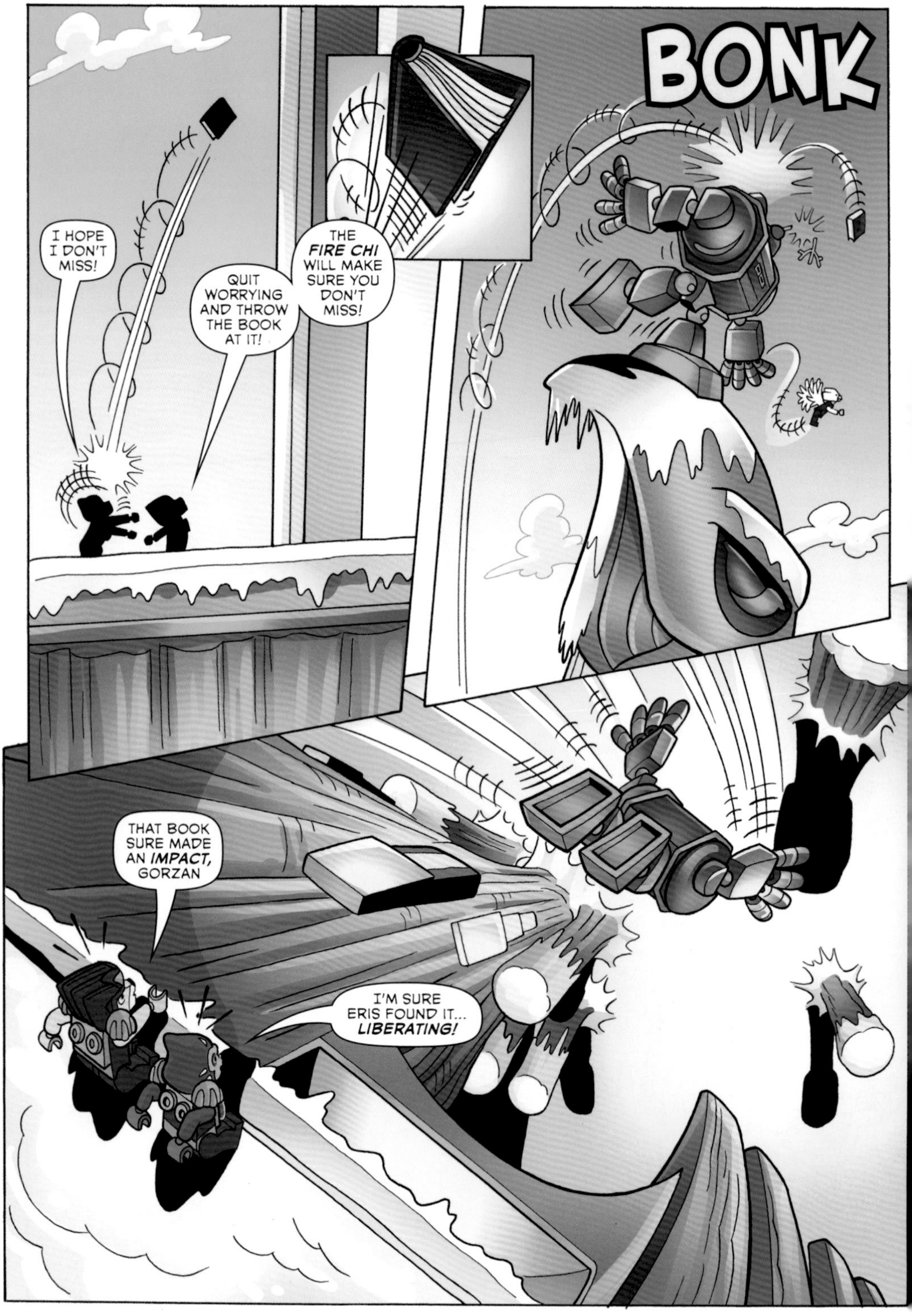
I HOPE I DON'T MISS!
QUIT WORRYING AND THROW THE BOOK AT IT!
THE *FIRE CHI* WILL MAKE SURE YOU DON'T MISS!
BONK
THAT BOOK SURE MADE AN *IMPACT,* GORZAN
I'M SURE ERIS FOUND IT... *LIBERATING!*

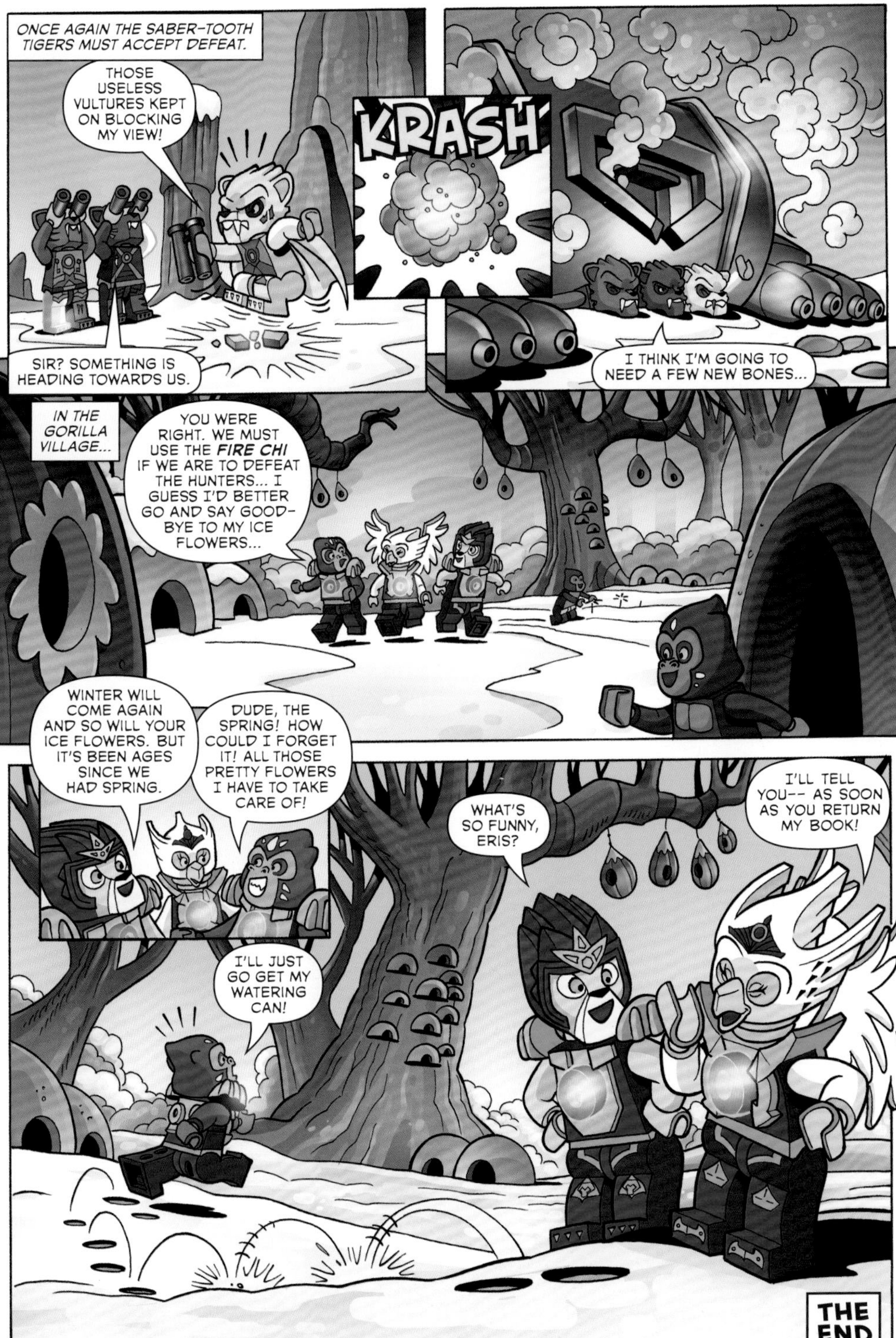

ONCE AGAIN THE SABER-TOOTH TIGERS MUST ACCEPT DEFEAT.
THOSE USELESS VULTURES KEPT ON BLOCKING MY VIEW!
SIR? SOMETHING IS HEADING TOWARDS US.
KRASH
I THINK I'M GOING TO NEED A FEW NEW BONES...
IN THE GORILLA VILLAGE...
YOU WERE RIGHT. WE MUST USE THE FIRE CHI IF WE ARE TO DEFEAT THE HUNTERS... I GUESS I'D BETTER GO AND SAY GOOD-BYE TO MY ICE FLOWERS...
WINTER WILL COME AGAIN AND SO WILL YOUR ICE FLOWERS. BUT IT'S BEEN AGES SINCE WE HAD SPRING.
DUDE, THE SPRING! HOW COULD I FORGET IT! ALL THOSE PRETTY FLOWERS I HAVE TO TAKE CARE OF!
WHAT'S SO FUNNY, ERIS?
I'LL TELL YOU-- AS SOON AS YOU RETURN MY BOOK!
I'LL JUST GO GET MY WATERING CAN!
THE END

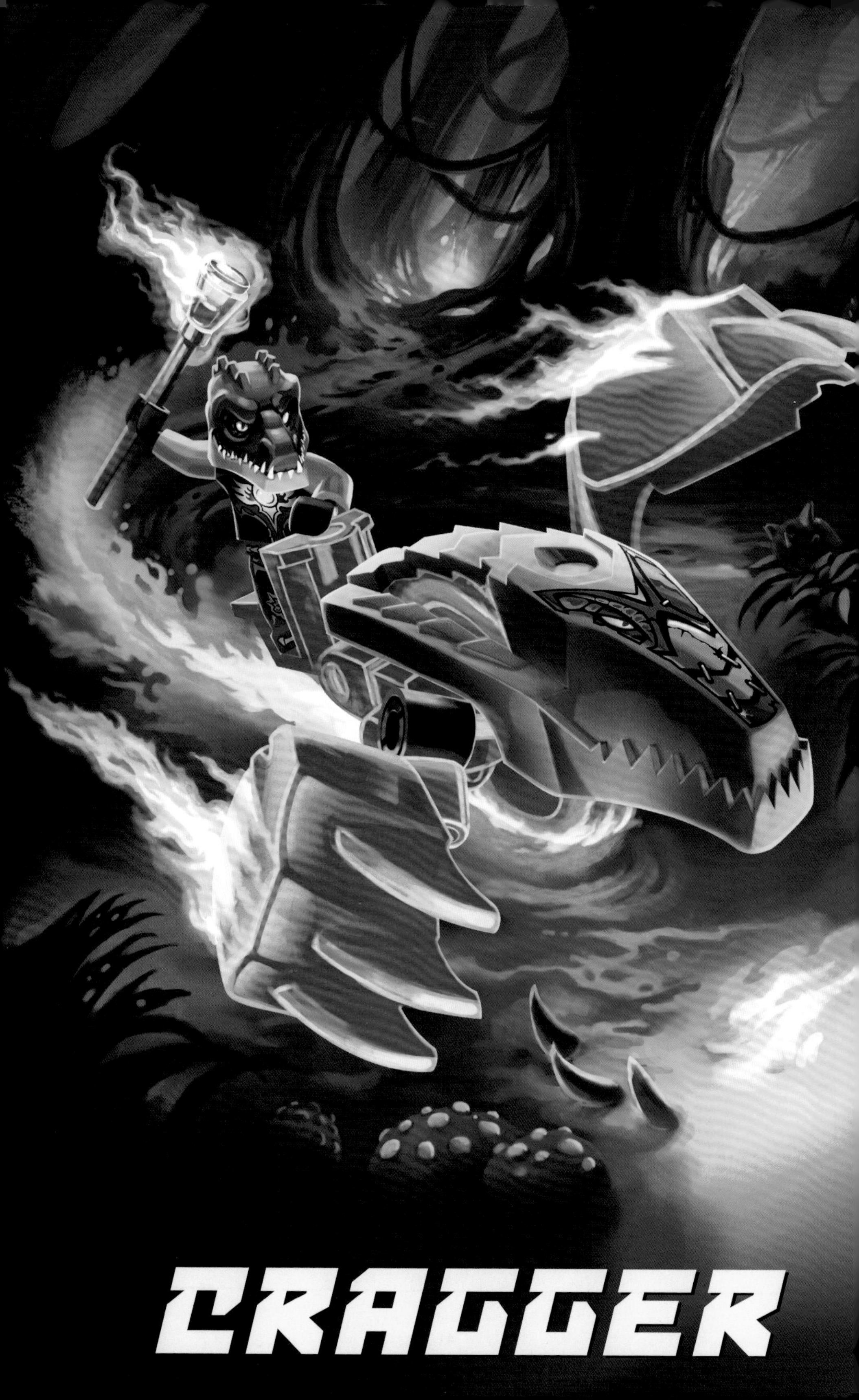
CRAGGER

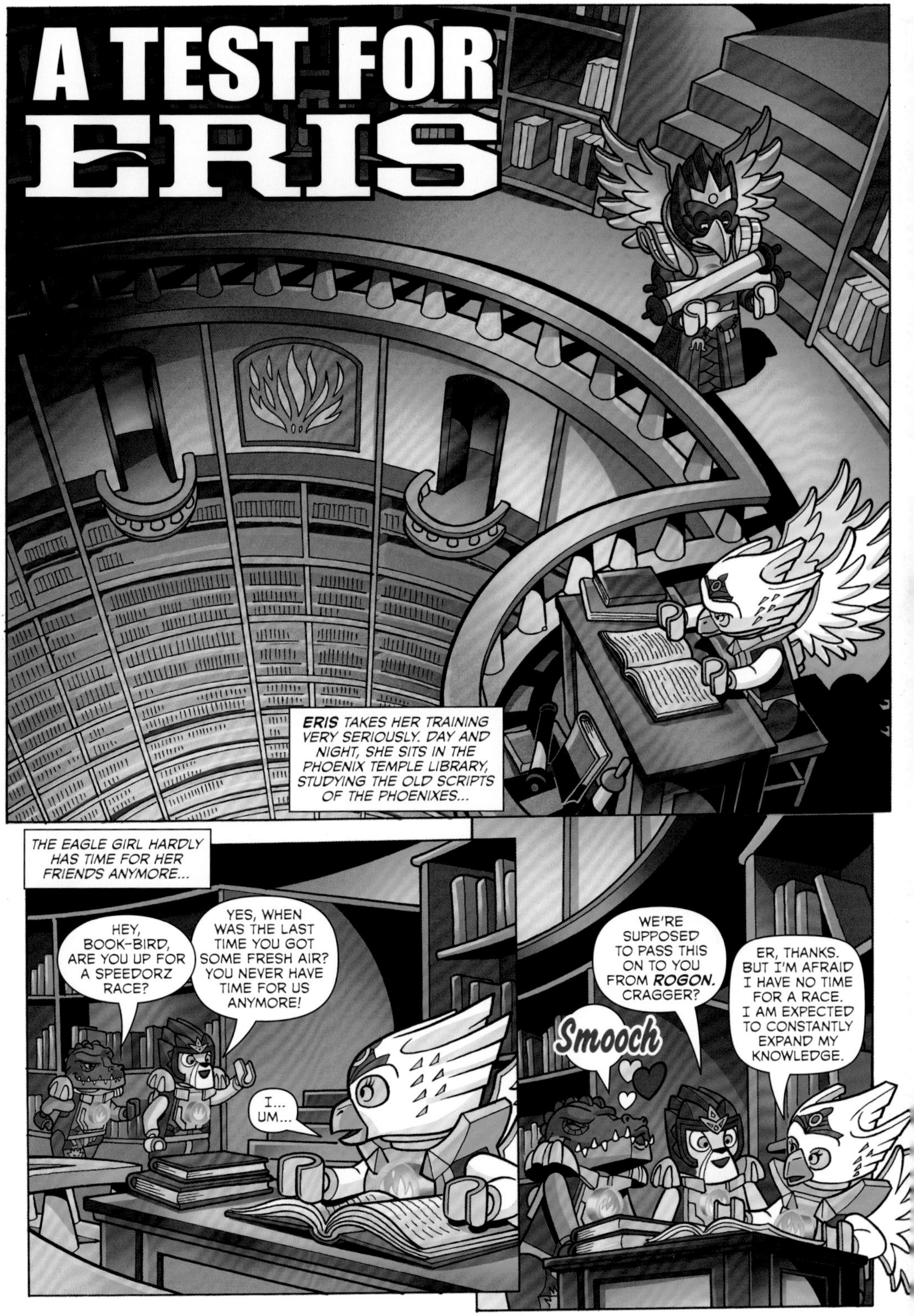
A TEST FOR ERIS
ERIS TAKES HER TRAINING VERY SERIOUSLY. DAY AND NIGHT, SHE SITS IN THE PHOENIX TEMPLE LIBRARY, STUDYING THE OLD SCRIPTS OF THE PHOENIXES...
THE EAGLE GIRL HARDLY HAS TIME FOR HER FRIENDS ANYMORE...
HEY, BOOK-BIRD, ARE YOU UP FOR A SPEEDORZ RACE?
YES, WHEN WAS THE LAST TIME YOU GOT SOME FRESH AIR? YOU NEVER HAVE TIME FOR US ANYMORE!
I... UM...
WE'RE SUPPOSED TO PASS THIS ON TO YOU FROM ROGON. CRAGGER?
Smooch
ER, THANKS. BUT I'M AFRAID I HAVE NO TIME FOR A RACE. I AM EXPECTED TO CONSTANTLY EXPAND MY KNOWLEDGE.

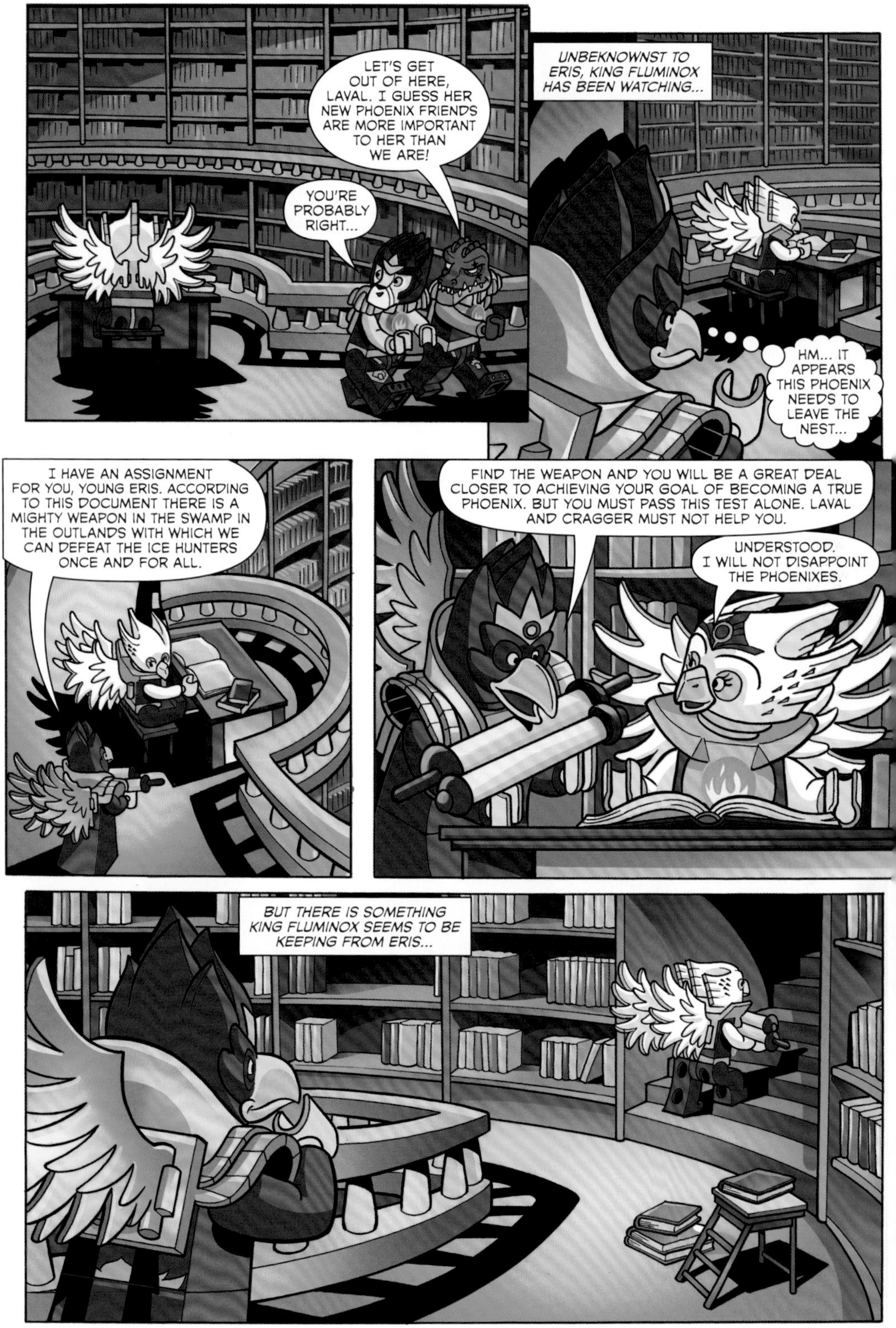
LET'S GET OUT OF HERE, LAVAL. I GUESS HER NEW PHOENIX FRIENDS ARE MORE IMPORTANT TO HER THAN WE ARE!
YOU'RE PROBABLY RIGHT...
UNBEKNOWNST TO ERIS, KING FLUMINOX HAS BEEN WATCHING...
HM... IT APPEARS THIS PHOENIX NEEDS TO LEAVE THE NEST...
I HAVE AN ASSIGNMENT FOR YOU, YOUNG ERIS. ACCORDING TO THIS DOCUMENT THERE IS A MIGHTY WEAPON IN THE SWAMP IN THE OUTLANDS WITH WHICH WE CAN DEFEAT THE ICE HUNTERS ONCE AND FOR ALL.
FIND THE WEAPON AND YOU WILL BE A GREAT DEAL CLOSER TO ACHIEVING YOUR GOAL OF BECOMING A TRUE PHOENIX. BUT YOU MUST PASS THIS TEST ALONE. LAVAL AND CRAGGER MUST NOT HELP YOU.
UNDERSTOOD. I WILL NOT DISAPPOINT THE PHOENIXES.
BUT THERE IS SOMETHING KING FLUMINOX SEEMS TO BE KEEPING FROM ERIS...

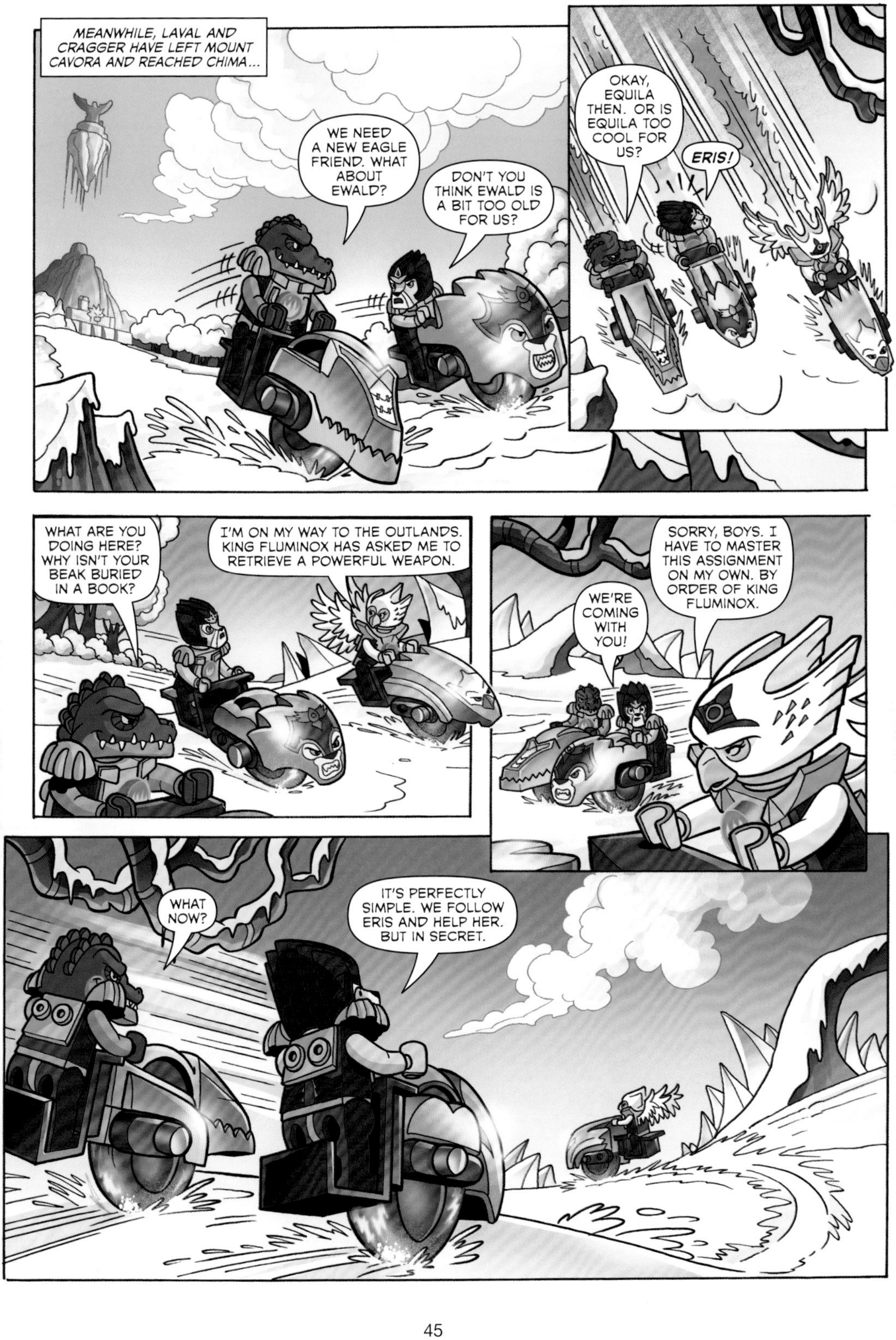
MEANWHILE, LAVAL AND CRAGGER HAVE LEFT MOUNT CAVORA AND REACHED CHIMA...
WE NEED A NEW EAGLE FRIEND. WHAT ABOUT EWALD?
DON'T YOU THINK EWALD IS A BIT TOO OLD FOR US?
OKAY, EQUILA THEN. OR IS EQUILA TOO COOL FOR US?
ERIS!
WHAT ARE YOU DOING HERE? WHY ISN'T YOUR BEAK BURIED IN A BOOK?
I'M ON MY WAY TO THE OUTLANDS. KING FLUMINOX HAS ASKED ME TO RETRIEVE A POWERFUL WEAPON.
WE'RE COMING WITH YOU!
SORRY, BOYS. I HAVE TO MASTER THIS ASSIGNMENT ON MY OWN. BY ORDER OF KING FLUMINOX.
WHAT NOW?
IT'S PERFECTLY SIMPLE. WE FOLLOW ERIS AND HELP HER. BUT IN SECRET.

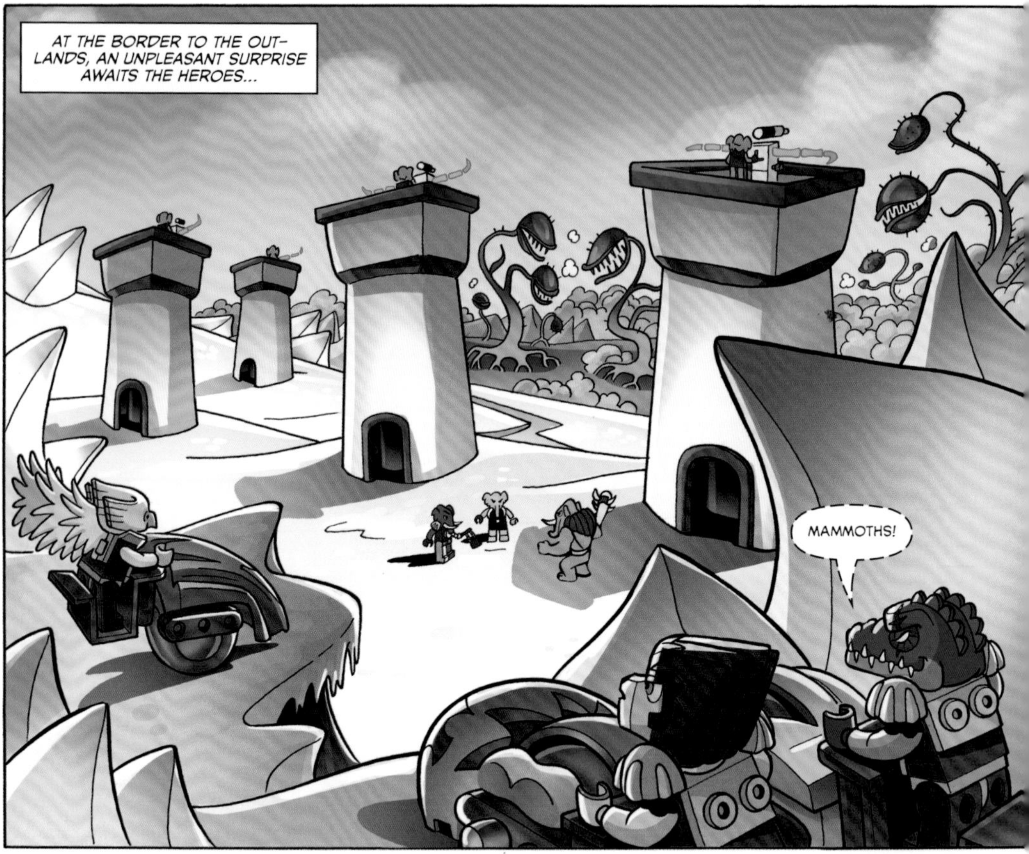
AT THE BORDER TO THE OUT-LANDS, AN UNPLEASANT SURPRISE AWAITS THE HEROES...
MAMMOTHS!

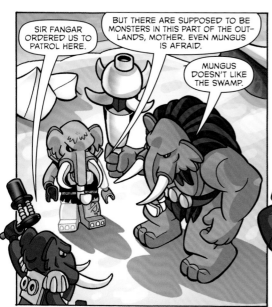

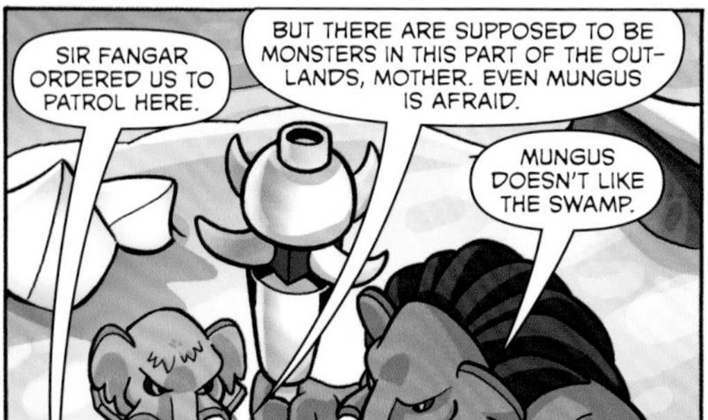
SIR FANGAR ORDERED US TO PATROL HERE.
BUT THERE ARE SUPPOSED TO BE MONSTERS IN THIS PART OF THE OUT-LANDS, MOTHER. EVEN MUNGUS IS AFRAID.
MUNGUS DOESN'T LIKE THE SWAMP.

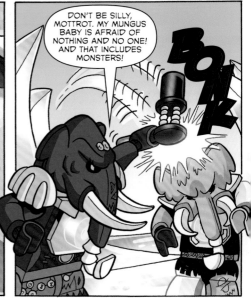

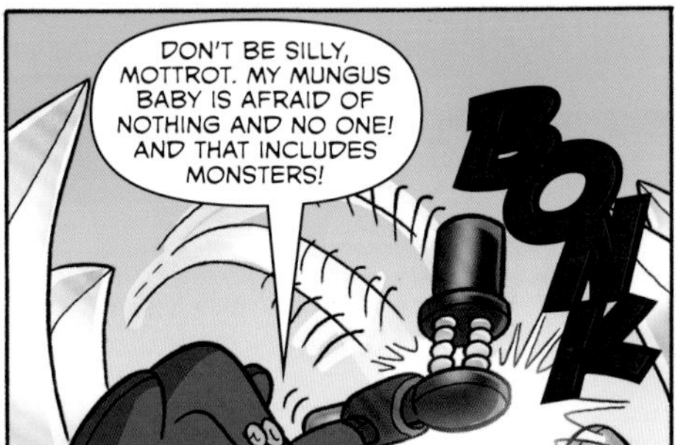
DON'T BE SILLY, MOTTROT. MY MUNGUS BABY IS AFRAID OF NOTHING AND NO ONE! AND THAT INCLUDES MONSTERS!
BONK

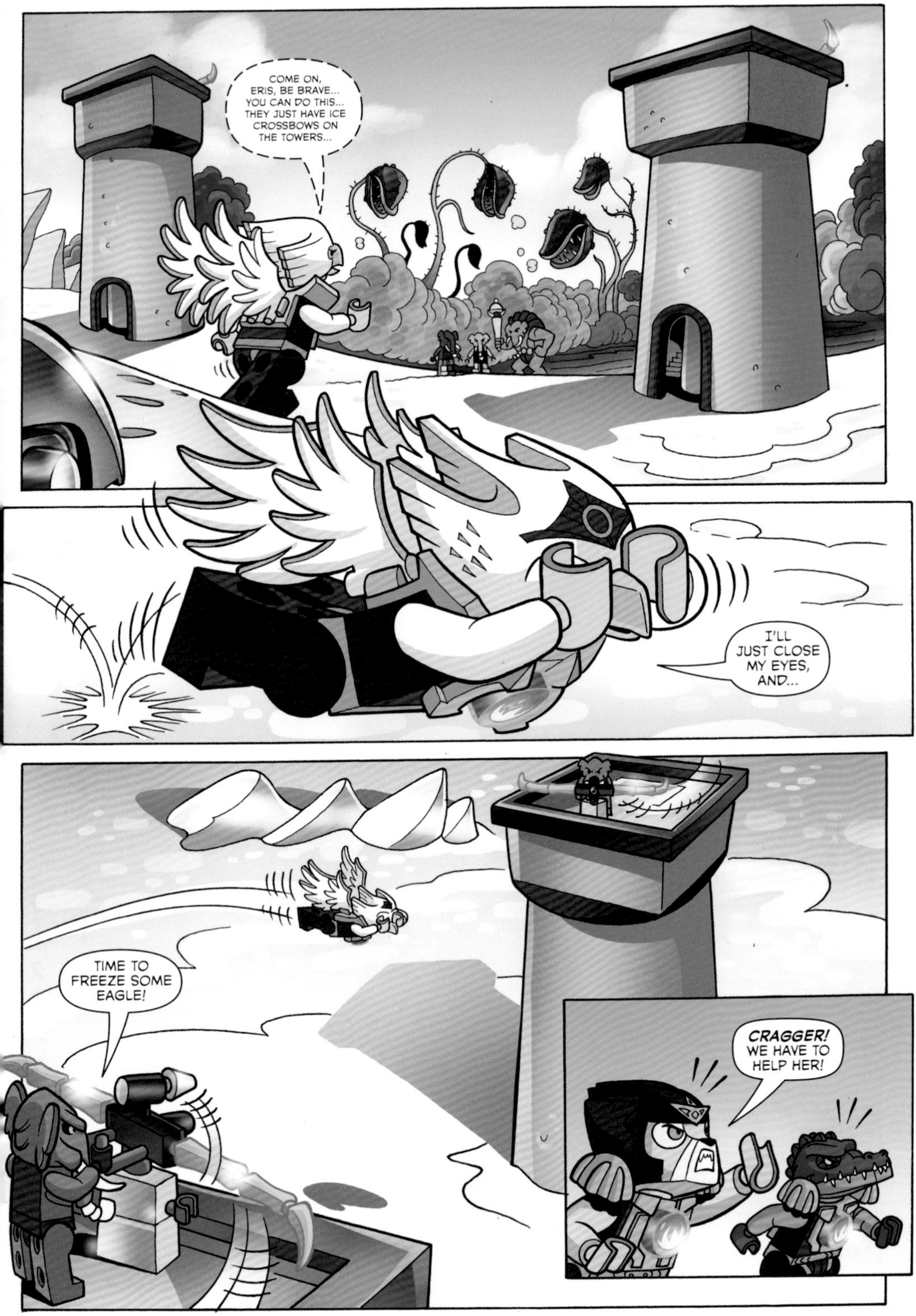
COME ON, ERIS, BE BRAVE... YOU CAN DO THIS... THEY JUST HAVE ICE CROSSBOWS ON THE TOWERS...
I'LL JUST CLOSE MY EYES, AND...
TIME TO FREEZE SOME EAGLE!
CRAGGER! WE HAVE TO HELP HER!

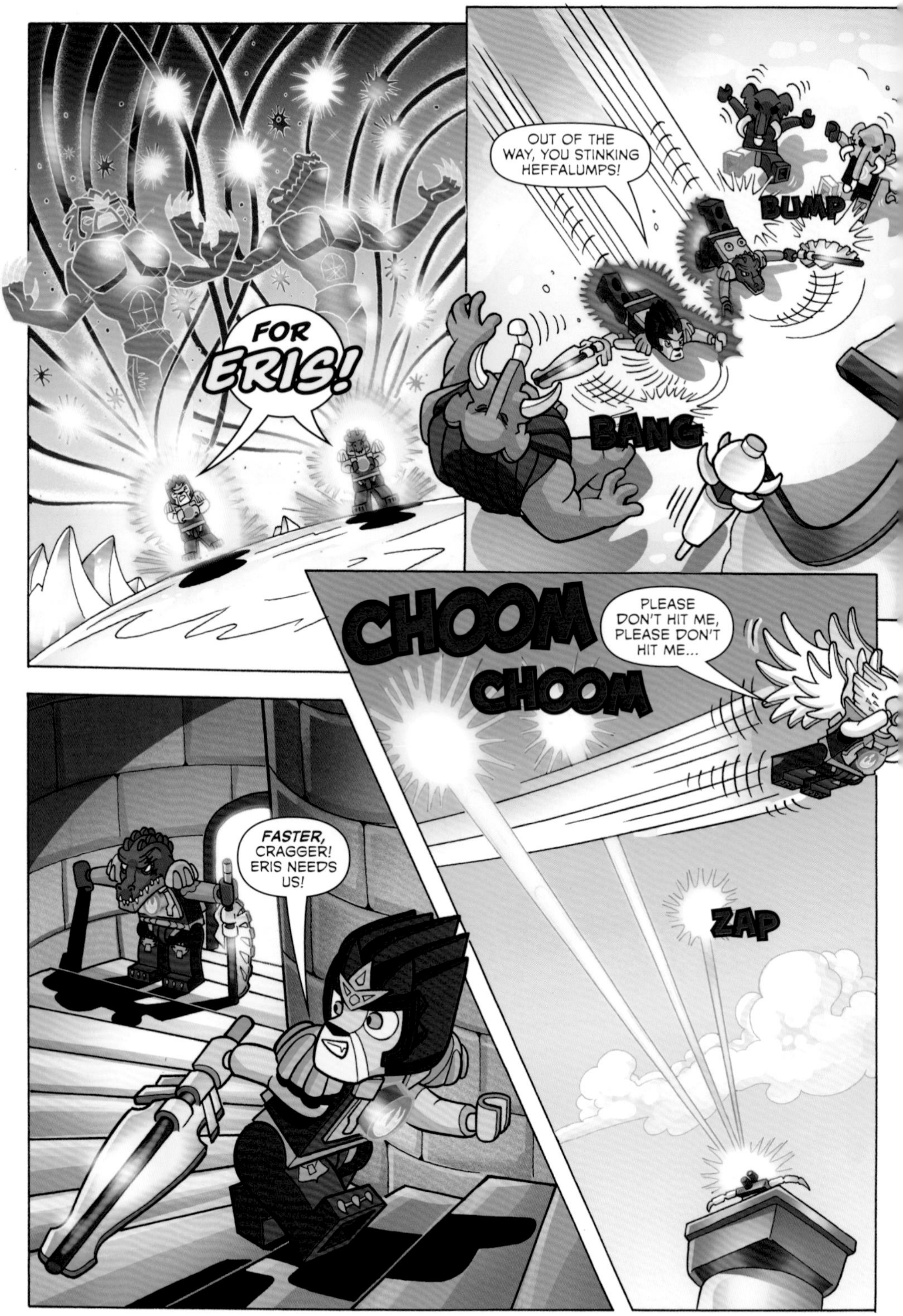
FOR ERIS!
OUT OF THE WAY, YOU STINKING HEFFALUMPS!
BUMP
BANG
CHOOM
CHOOM
PLEASE DON'T HIT ME, PLEASE DON'T HIT ME...
FASTER, CRAGGER! ERIS NEEDS US!
ZAP

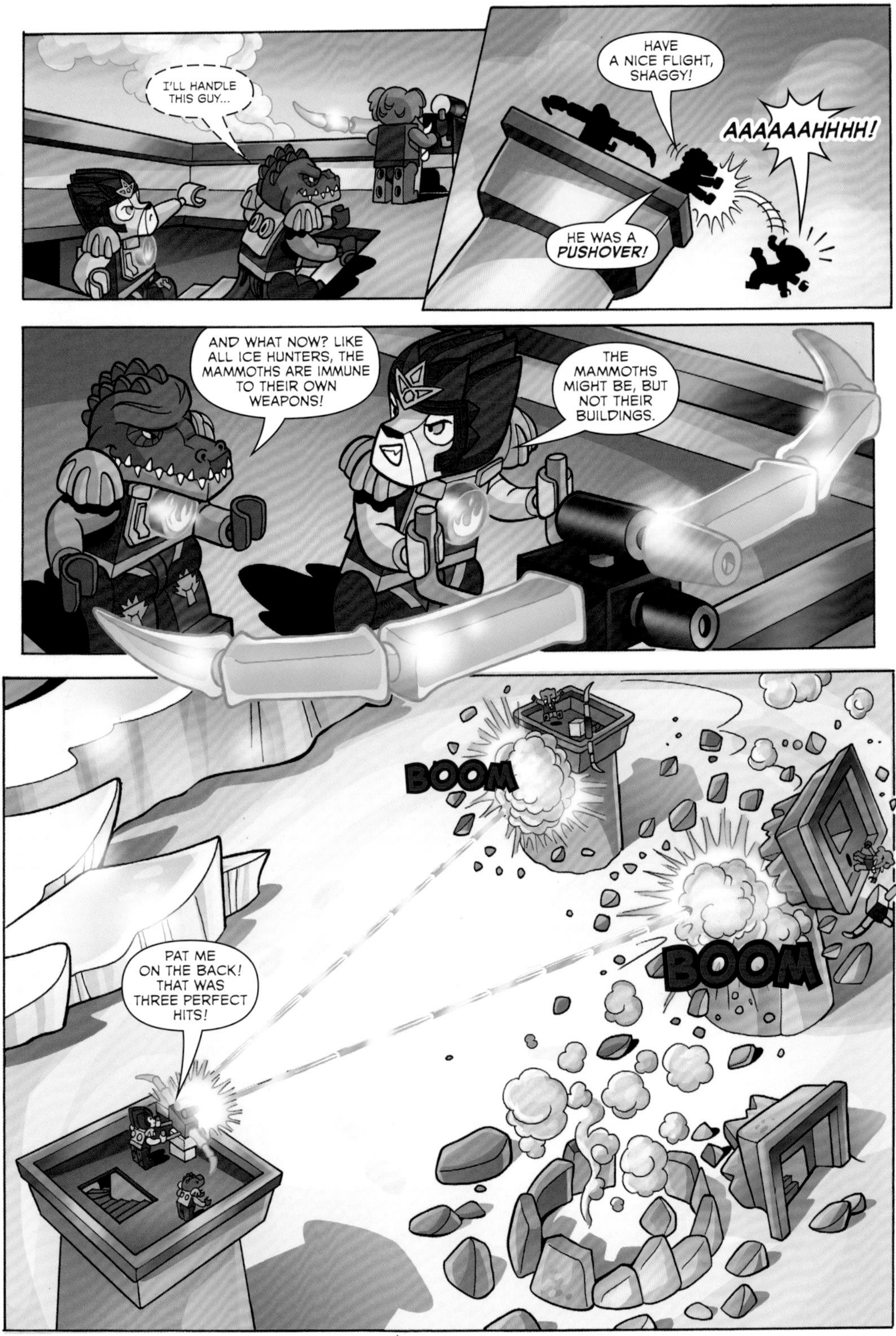
I'LL HANDLE THIS GUY...
HAVE A NICE FLIGHT, SHAGGY!
HE WAS A PUSHOVER!
AAAAAAHHHH!
AND WHAT NOW? LIKE ALL ICE HUNTERS, THE MAMMOTHS ARE IMMUNE TO THEIR OWN WEAPONS!
THE MAMMOTHS MIGHT BE, BUT NOT THEIR BUILDINGS.
BOOM
BOOM
PAT ME ON THE BACK! THAT WAS THREE PERFECT HITS!

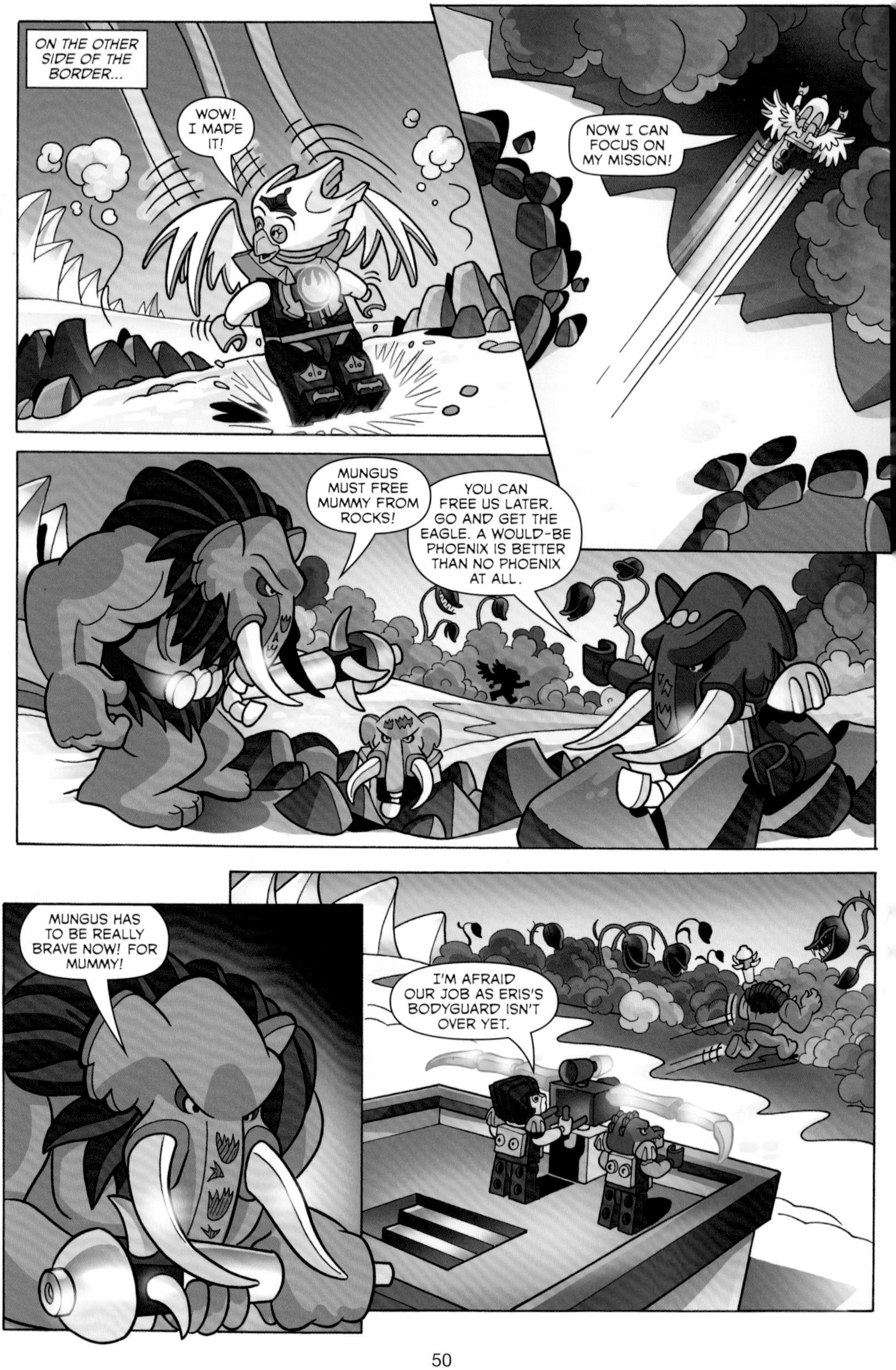
ON THE OTHER SIDE OF THE BORDER...
WOW! I MADE IT!
NOW I CAN FOCUS ON MY MISSION!
MUNGUS MUST FREE MUMMY FROM ROCKS!
YOU CAN FREE US LATER. GO AND GET THE EAGLE. A WOULD-BE PHOENIX IS BETTER THAN NO PHOENIX AT ALL.
MUNGUS HAS TO BE REALLY BRAVE NOW! FOR MUMMY!
I'M AFRAID OUR JOB AS ERIS'S BODYGUARD ISN'T OVER YET.

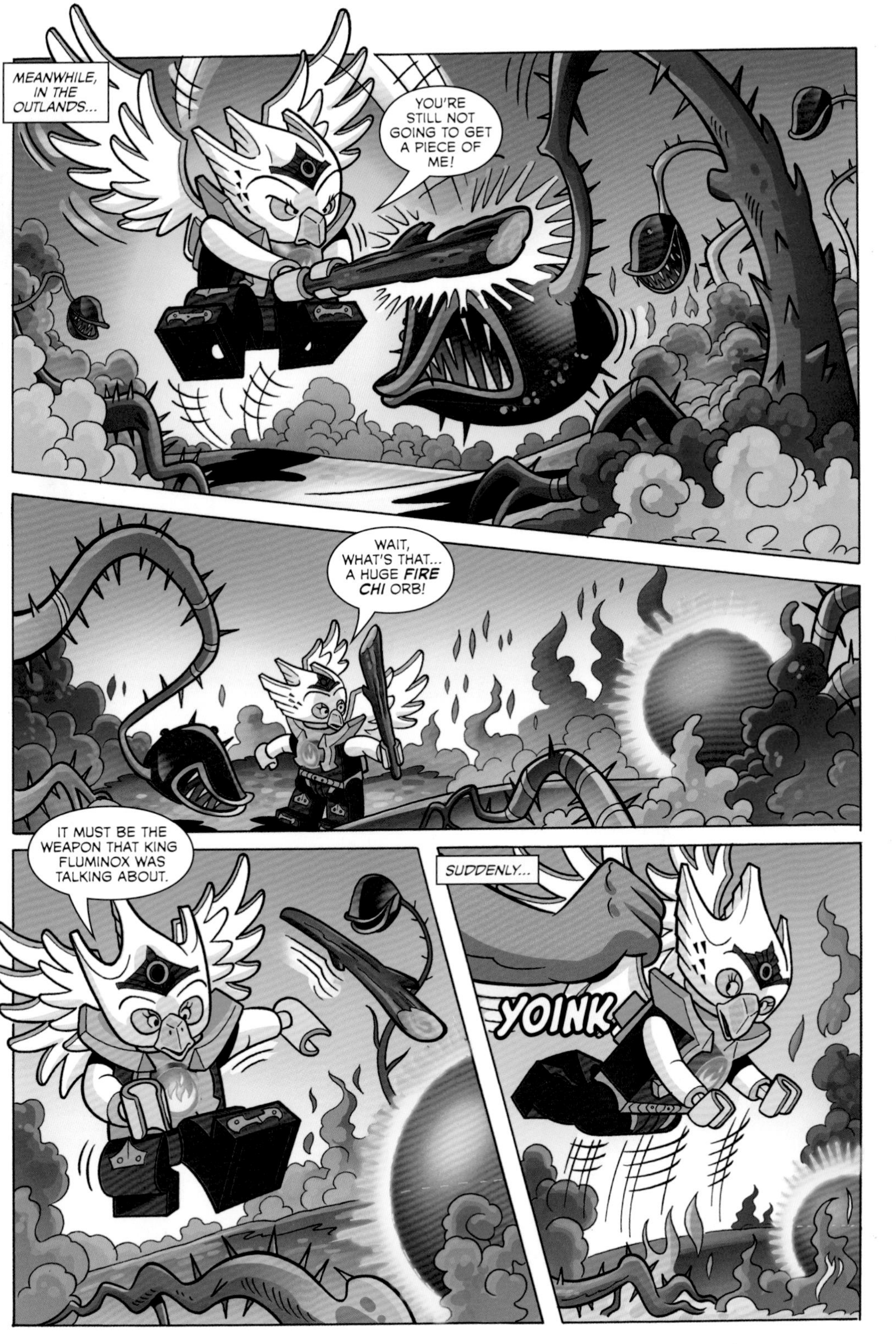
MEANWHILE, IN THE OUTLANDS...
YOU'RE STILL NOT GOING TO GET A PIECE OF ME!
WAIT, WHAT'S THAT... A HUGE FIRE CHI ORB!
IT MUST BE THE WEAPON THAT KING FLUMINOX WAS TALKING ABOUT.
SUDDENLY...
YOINK.

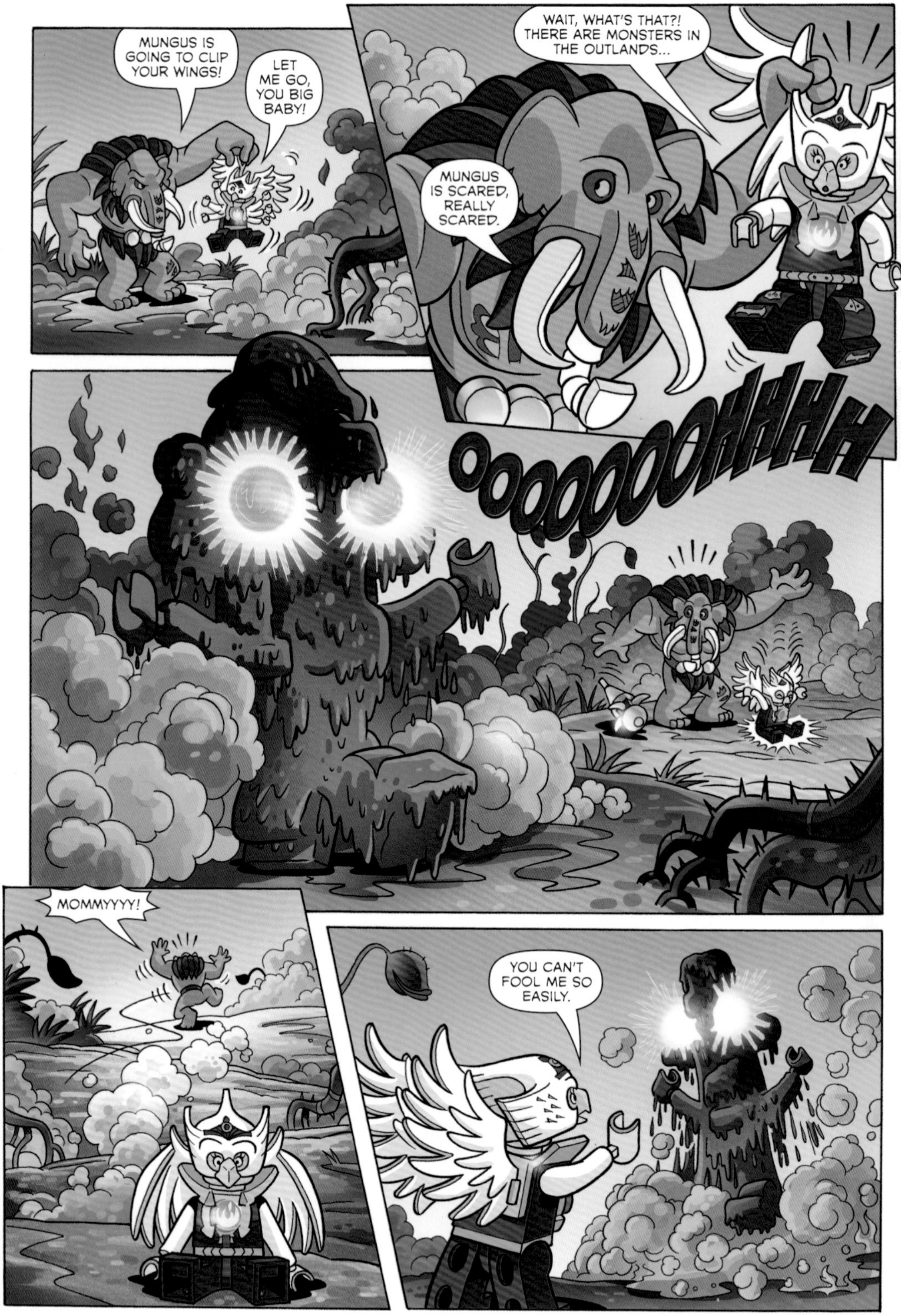
MUNGUS IS GOING TO CLIP YOUR WINGS!
LET ME GO, YOU BIG BABY!
WAIT, WHAT'S THAT?! THERE ARE MONSTERS IN THE OUTLANDS...
MUNGUS IS SCARED, REALLY SCARED.
OOOOOOOOOHHHHH
MOMMYYYY!
YOU CAN'T FOOL ME SO EASILY.

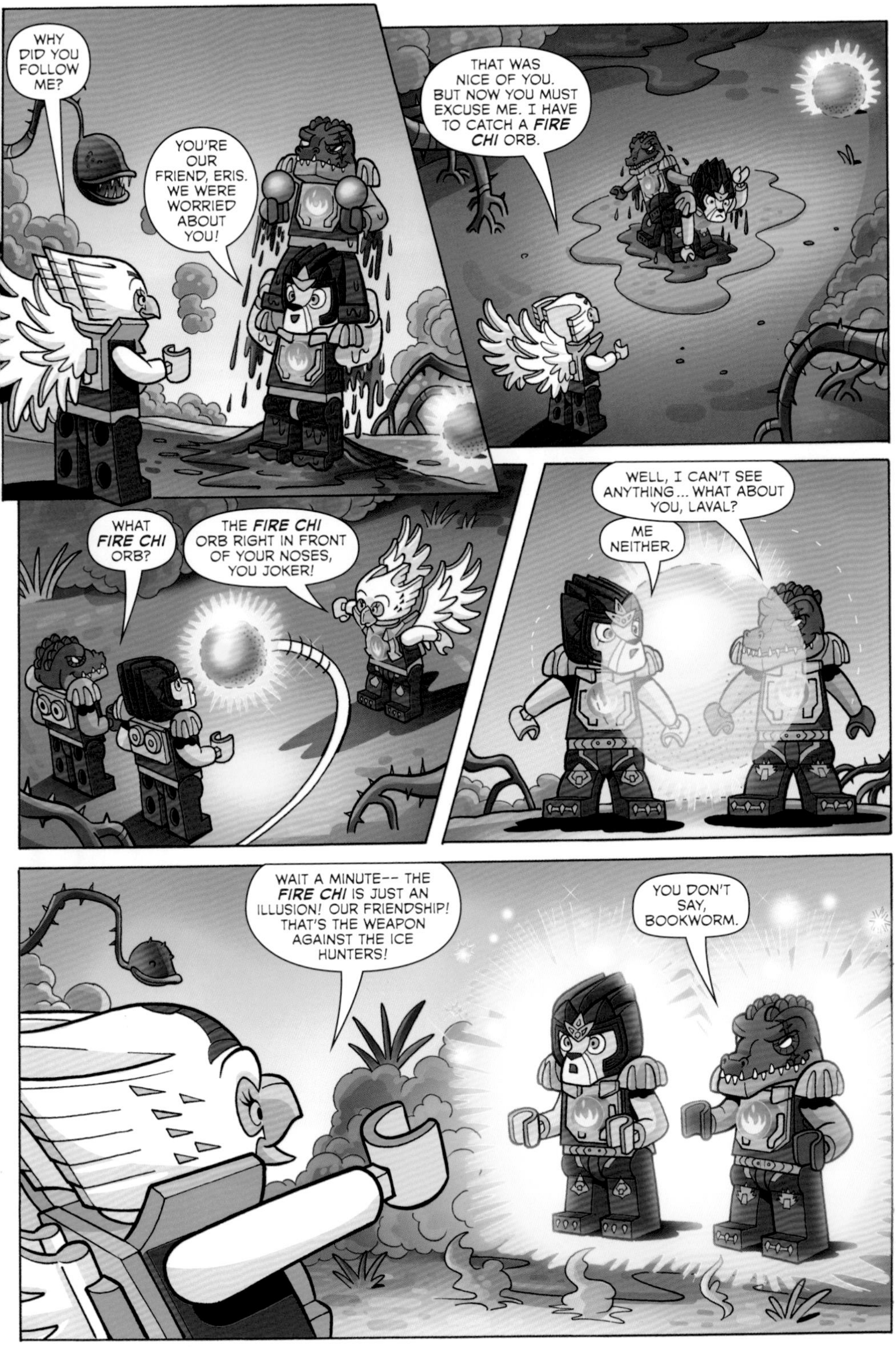
WHY DID YOU FOLLOW ME?
YOU'RE OUR FRIEND, ERIS. WE WERE WORRIED ABOUT YOU!
THAT WAS NICE OF YOU. BUT NOW YOU MUST EXCUSE ME. I HAVE TO CATCH A FIRE CHI ORB.
WHAT FIRE CHI ORB?
THE FIRE CHI ORB RIGHT IN FRONT OF YOUR NOSES, YOU JOKER!
WELL, I CAN'T SEE ANYTHING... WHAT ABOUT YOU, LAVAL?
ME NEITHER.
WAIT A MINUTE-- THE FIRE CHI IS JUST AN ILLUSION! OUR FRIENDSHIP! THAT'S THE WEAPON AGAINST THE ICE HUNTERS!
YOU DON'T SAY, BOOKWORM.

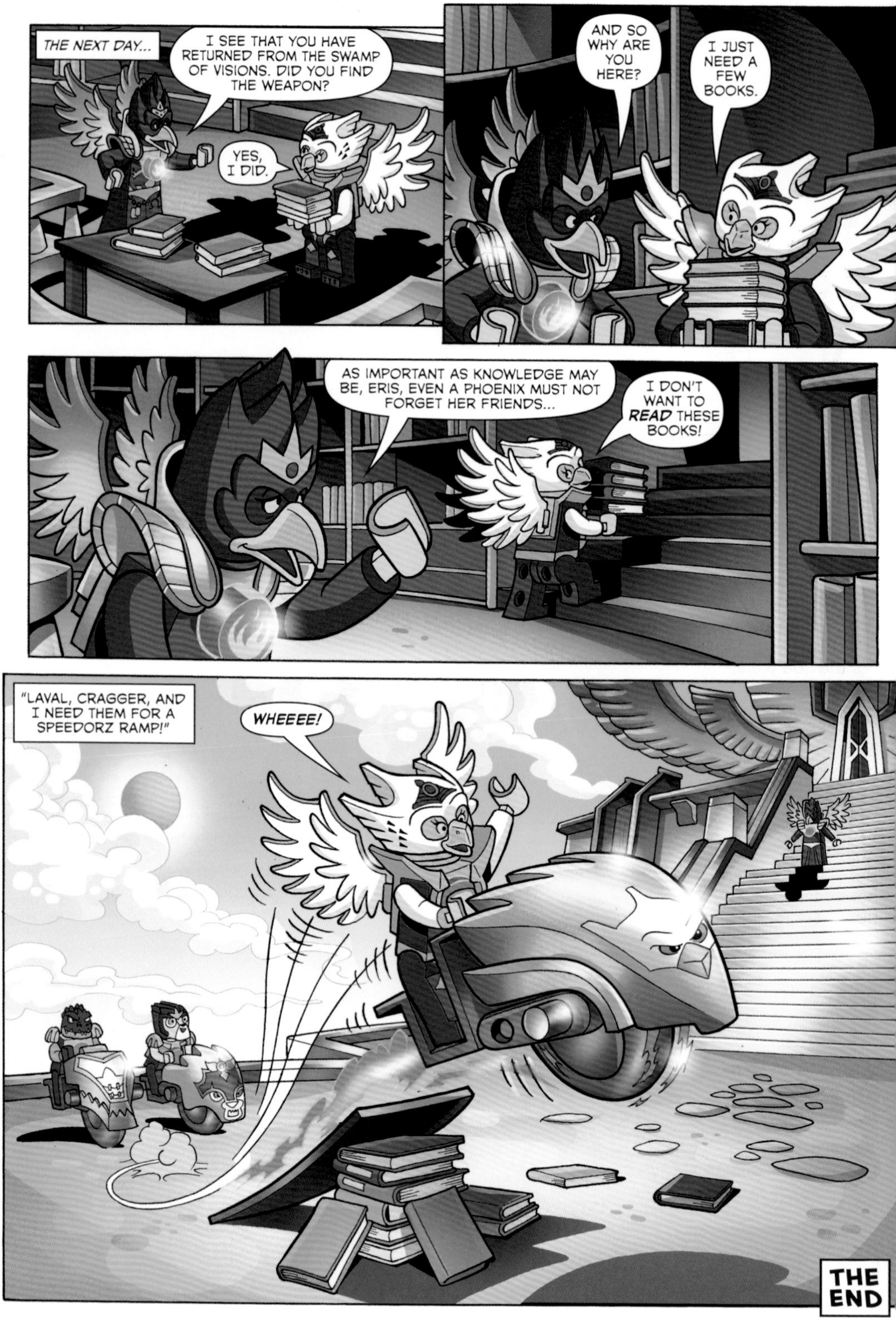
THE NEXT DAY...
I SEE THAT YOU HAVE RETURNED FROM THE SWAMP OF VISIONS. DID YOU FIND THE WEAPON?
YES, I DID.
AND SO WHY ARE YOU HERE?
I JUST NEED A FEW BOOKS.
AS IMPORTANT AS KNOWLEDGE MAY BE, ERIS, EVEN A PHOENIX MUST NOT FORGET HER FRIENDS...
I DON'T WANT TO READ THESE BOOKS!
"LAVAL, CRAGGER, AND I NEED THEM FOR A SPEEDORZ RAMP!"
WHEEEE!
THE END

WATCH OUT FOR PAPERCUTZ™

Welcome to the Fire CHI-filled fourth LEGO® LEGENDS OF CHIMA graphic novel, by Yannick Grotholt and Comicon, from Papercutz—those chia tea-drinking guys dedicated to publishing great graphic novels for all ages. I'm Jim Salicrup, the de-constructible Editor-in-Chief and part-time librarian for the Phoenixes ! I'm here to take a little look back at all the LEGO graphic novel series available to you from Papercutz.

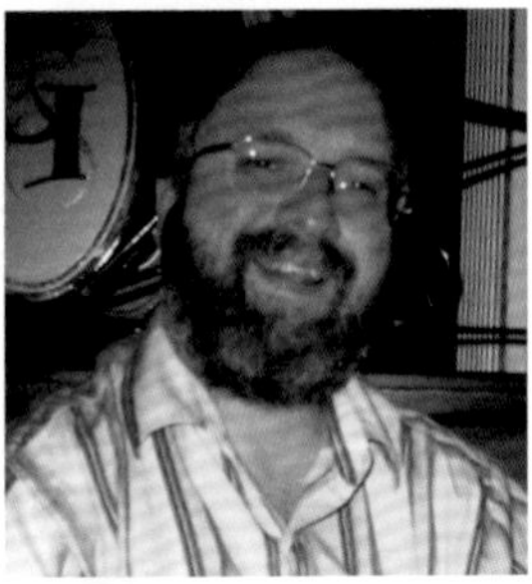

Of course, it all started with LEGO® BIONICLE. These digest-sized graphic novels featured the great comics that were originally created by DC Comics and were included in the BIONICLE canisters or in the LEGO Fan Club magazine. Every single comics story we published was written by the super-talented Greg Farshtey, including the all-new stories created just for Papercutz. In the Papercutz blog, and in the Watch Out for Papercutz page in BIONICLE #8 "Legends of Bara Magna," Greg revealed the behind-the-scenes story of how BIONICLE was created. In case you missed that fascinating tale, allow me to share it with you again...

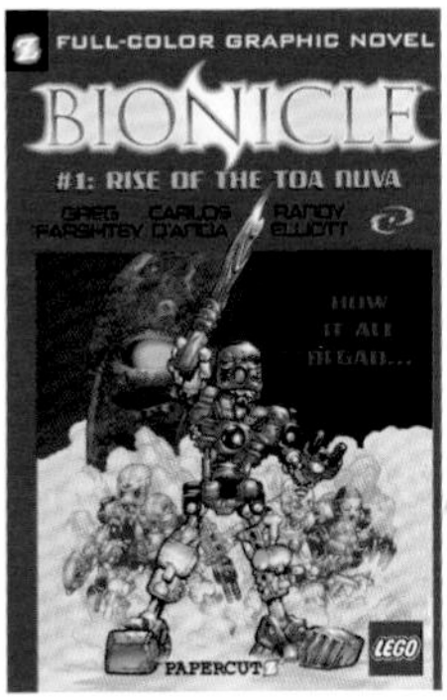
FULL-COLOR GRAPHIC NOVEL
BIONICLE
#1: RISE OF THE TOA NUVA
PAPERCUTZ
LEGO

"BIONICLE got its start in 1999-2000, when an international team of people employed by the Lego Group were tasked with coming up with a storyline-based LEGO line. The early working title was, believe it or not, 'Bone-Heads of Voodoo Island.' The first story bible (a summary of the year's story) for 2001 actually ended with Mata Nui awakening! No one could be sure if the BIONICLE stories would be big enough to last for more than one year...

"The BIONICLE line was introduced with a comicbook, truck tours, a 'build your own website' contest, and of course, the first six canister sets. The six villager sets (who would later come to be called 'Matoran') were available only through a McDonalds promotion.

"As the Toa were originally planned, they were all different ages and they would all sound sort of 'godlike' when they spoke. I had a long conversation with story team head Bob Thompson as I worked on the first comic, and suggested that the characters might be easier to relate to if they had different personalities, and spoke differently from each other, rather than all sounding like Thor or Superman. He agreed and that's how the initial characters were born in print."

Greg not only wrote all nine of the BIONICLE graphic novels published by Papercutz, he also wrote two in-depth guidebooks to the complex BIONICLES universe, reflecting two very different points of view—MATA NUI'S GUIDE TO BARA MAGNA and MAKUTA'S GUIDE TO THE UNIVERSE. Both profusely illustrated guidebooks were rare examples of books published by Papercutz not containing any comics! With a world as fantastic as the one depicted in the LEGO BIONICLE series, we seriously suspect we haven't seen the last of it!

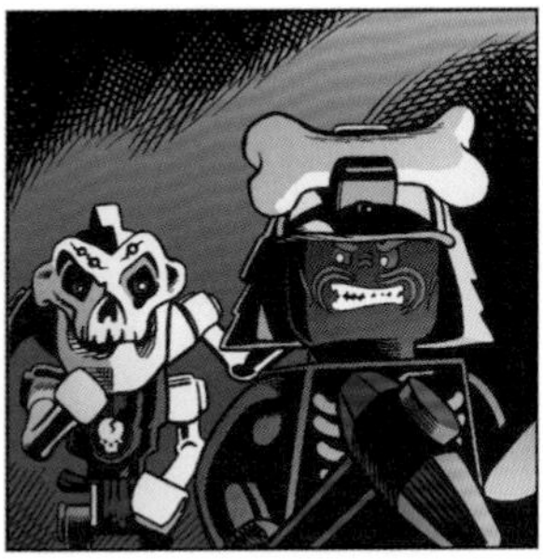

Of course, Greg then went on to write the hit LEGO NINJAGO graphic novel series for Papercutz, which was incredibly illustrated by PH Henrique and Jolyon Yates. When we look at Garmadon and Samukai, we wonder if perhaps they weren't somehow inspired by the "Bone-Heads of Voodoo Island"! Finally, we also published LEGO LEGENDS OF CHIMA™ written by Yannick Grotholt and beautifully illustrated by the team of artists known collectively as Comicon. We're incredibly proud of each and every LEGO graphic novel we've published and hope you've enjoyed them. If you missed any, you can still find them from your favorite bookseller or as e-books from comiXology.com or other e-book sellers.

From all of us at Papercutz, we sincerely thank you for your support. And don't miss THE LEGENDS OF CHIMA #5 -Coming Soon!

Thanks,

Jim

Bone-Head of Manhattan Island

STAY IN TOUCH!

EMAIL:	salicrup@papercutz.com
WEB:	papercutz.com
TWITTER:	@papercutzgn
FACEBOOK:	PAPERCUTZGRAPHICNOVELS
FAN MAIL:	Papercutz, 160 Broadway, Suite 700, East Wing, New York, NY 10038

LEGO® GRAPHIC NOVELS AVAILABLE FROM PAPERCUTZ™

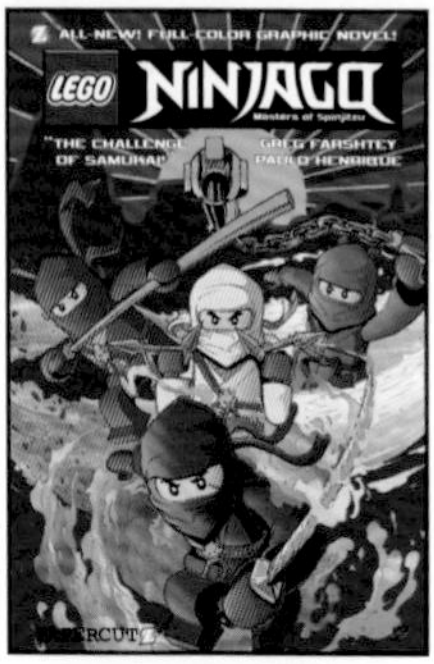
ALL-NEW! FULL-COLOR GRAPHIC NOVEL!
LEGO NINJAGO
"THE CHALLENGE OF SAMURAI"
GREG FARSHTEY
PAULO HENRIQUE
PAPERCUTZ
LEGO NINJAGO #1

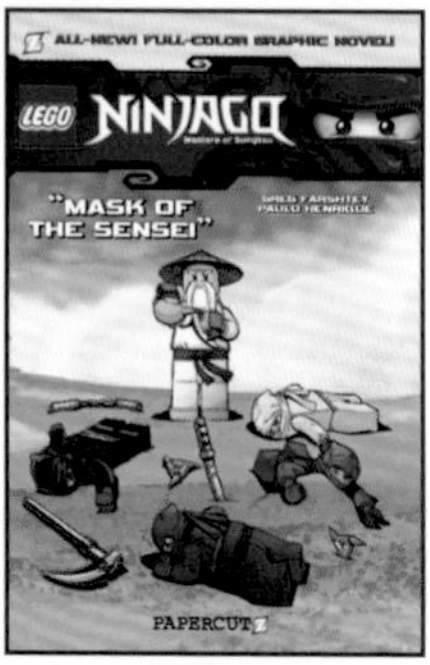
ALL-NEW! FULL-COLOR GRAPHIC NOVEL!
LEGO NINJAGO
"MASK OF THE SENSEI"
GREG FARSHTEY
PAULO HENRIQUE
PAPERCUTZ
LEGO NINJAGO #2

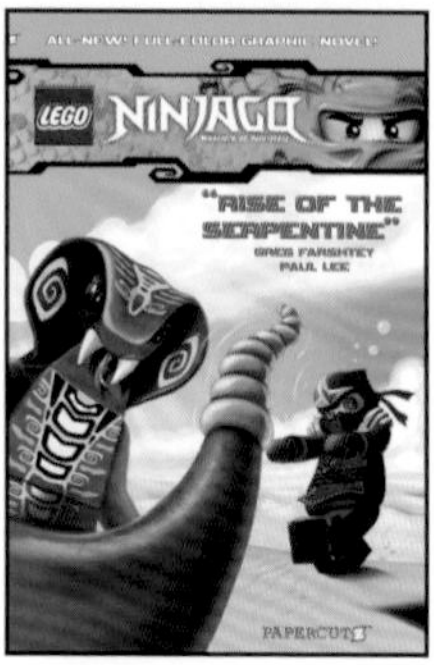
ALL-NEW! FULL-COLOR GRAPHIC NOVEL!
LEGO NINJAGO
"RISE OF THE SERPENTINE"
GREG FARSHTEY
PAUL LEE
PAPERCUTZ
LEGO NINJAGO #3

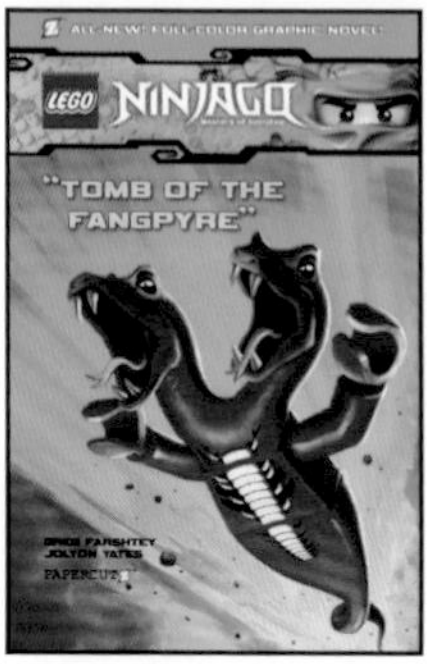
ALL-NEW! FULL-COLOR GRAPHIC NOVEL!
LEGO NINJAGO
"TOMB OF THE FANGPYRE"
GREG FARSHTEY
JOLYON YATES
PAPERCUTZ
LEGO NINJAGO #4

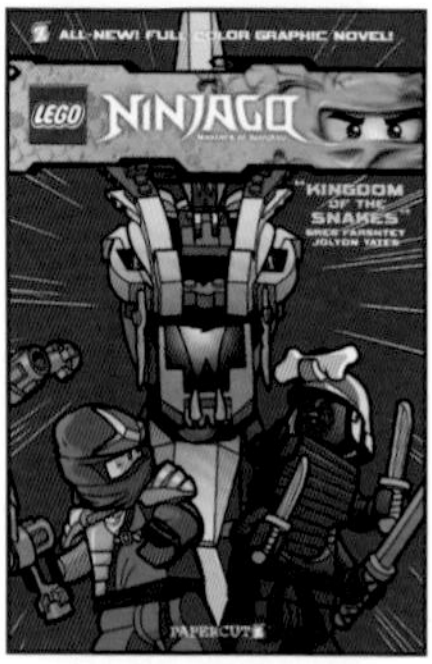
ALL-NEW! FULL-COLOR GRAPHIC NOVEL!
LEGO NINJAGO
"KINGDOM OF THE SNAKES"
GREG FARSHTEY
JOLYON YATES
PAPERCUTZ
LEGO NINJAGO #5

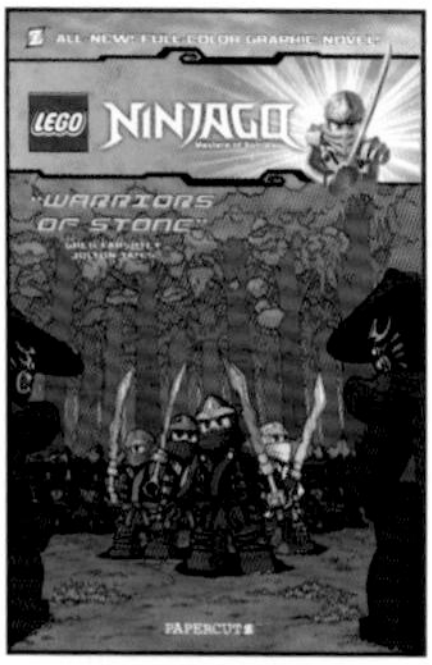
ALL-NEW! FULL-COLOR GRAPHIC NOVEL!
LEGO NINJAGO
"WARRIORS OF STONE"
PAPERCUTZ
LEGO NINJAGO #6

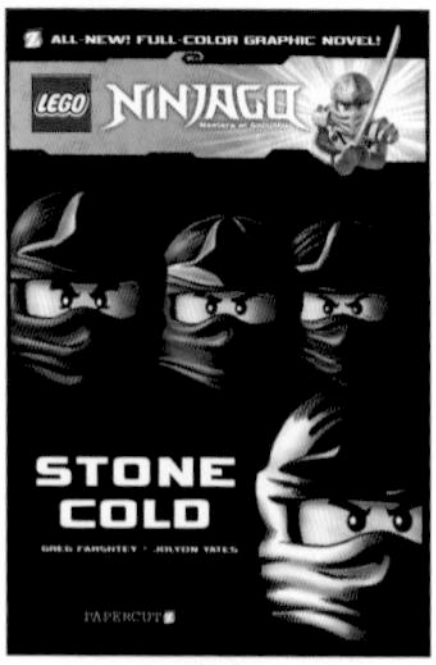
ALL-NEW! FULL-COLOR GRAPHIC NOVEL!
LEGO NINJAGO
STONE COLD
GREG FARSHTEY • JOLYON YATES
PAPERCUTZ
LEGO NINJAGO #7

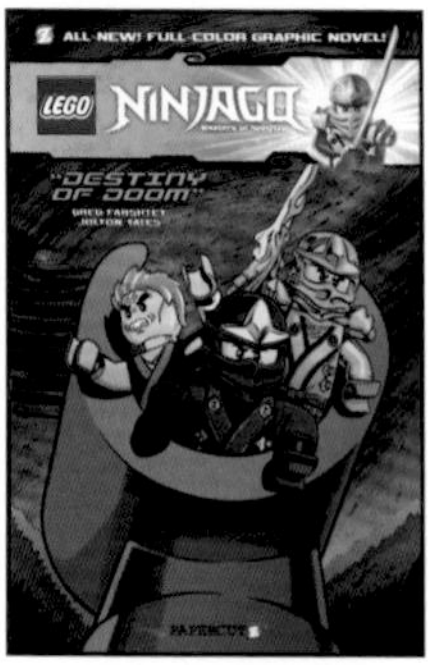
ALL-NEW! FULL-COLOR GRAPHIC NOVEL!
LEGO NINJAGO
"DESTINY OF DOOM"
GREG FARSHTEY
JOLYON YATES
PAPERCUTZ
LEGO NINJAGO #8

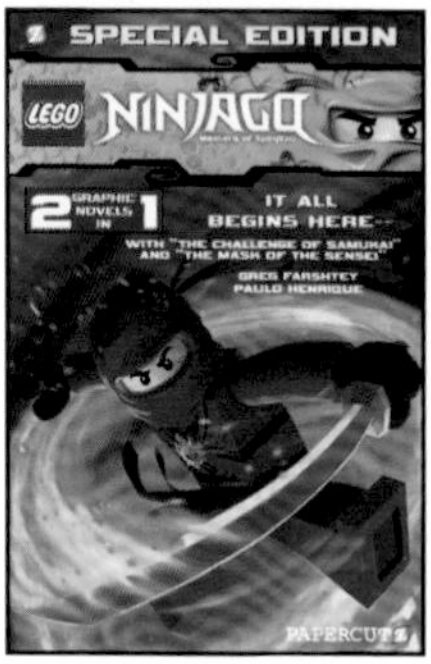
SPECIAL EDITION
LEGO NINJAGO
2 GRAPHIC NOVELS IN 1
IT ALL BEGINS HERE–
WITH "THE CHALLENGE OF SAMURAI" AND "THE MASK OF THE SENSEI"
GREG FARSHTEY
PAULO HENRIQUE
PAPERCUTZ
SPECIAL EDITION #1
(Features stories from LEGO NINJAGO #1 & #2.)

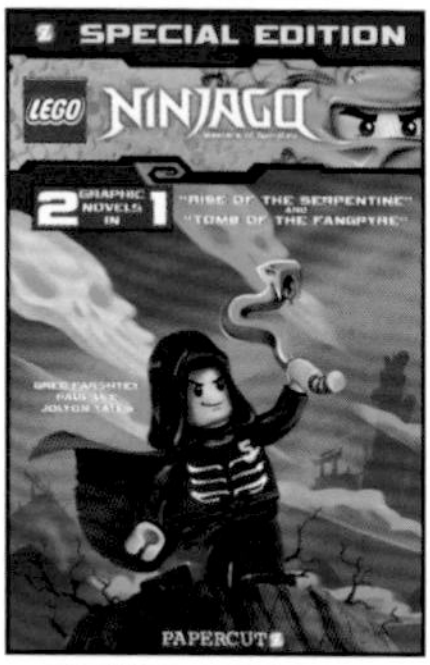
SPECIAL EDITION
LEGO NINJAGO
2 GRAPHIC NOVELS IN 1
"RISE OF THE SERPENTINE" AND "TOMB OF THE FANGPYRE"
PAPERCUTZ
SPECIAL EDITION #2
(Features stories from LEGO NINJAGO #3 & #4.)

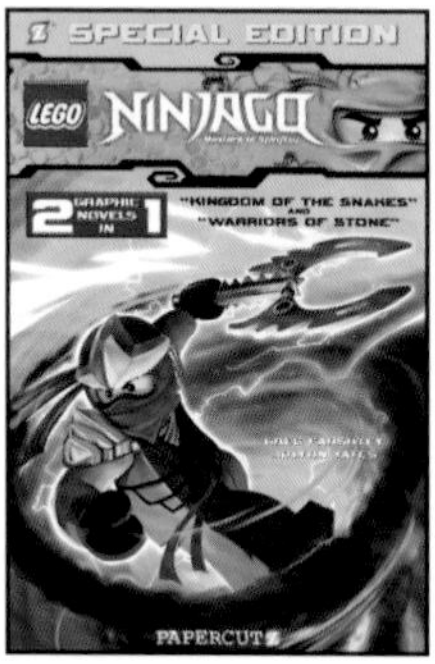
SPECIAL EDITION
LEGO NINJAGO
2 GRAPHIC NOVELS IN 1
"KINGDOM OF THE SNAKES" AND "WARRIORS OF STONE"
PAPERCUTZ
SPECIAL EDITION #3
(Features stories from LEGO NINJAGO #5 & #6.)

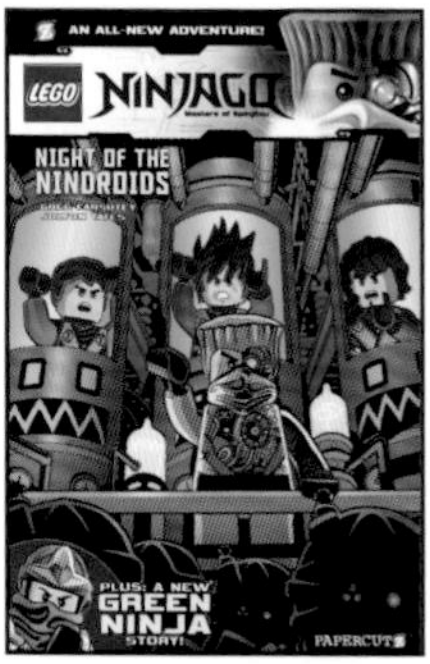
AN ALL-NEW ADVENTURE!
LEGO NINJAGO
NIGHT OF THE NINDROIDS
PLUS: A NEW GREEN NINJA STORY!
PAPERCUTZ
LEGO NINJAGO #9

LEGO® NINJAGO™ graphic novels are available in paperback and hardcover at booksellers everywhere.

LEGO® NINJAGO #1-11 are $6.99 in paperback, and $10.99 in hardcover. LEGO NINJAGO SPECIAL EDITION #1-3 are $10.99 in paperback only. You can also order online at papercutz.com. Or call 1-800-886-1223, Monday through Friday, 9 – 5 EST. MC, Visa, and AmEx accepted. To order by mail, please add $4.00 for postage and handling for first book ordered, $1.00 for each additional book and make check payable to NBM Publishing. Send to: Papercutz, 160 Broadway, Suite 700, East Wing, New York, NY 10038.

LEGO NINJAGO graphic novels are also available digitally wherever e-books are sold.

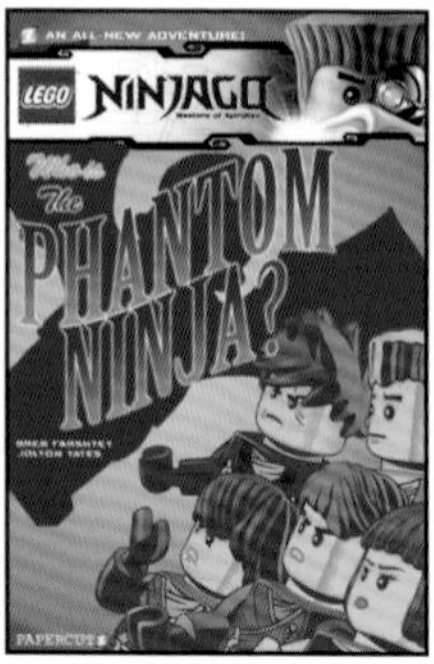
AN ALL-NEW ADVENTURE!
LEGO NINJAGO
Who is The PHANTOM NINJA?
GREG FARSHTEY
JOLYON YATES
PAPERCUTZ
LEGO NINJAGO #10

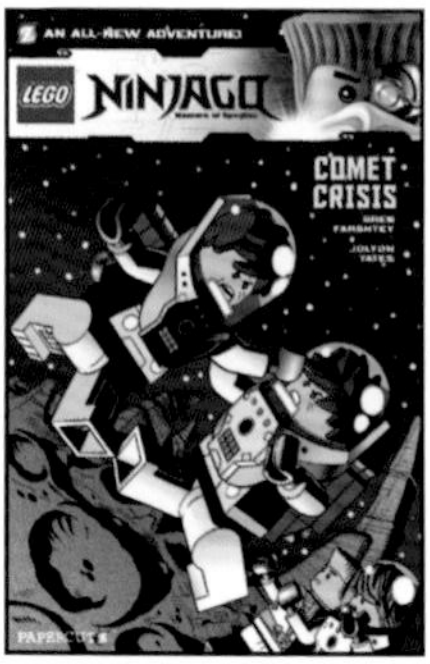
AN ALL-NEW ADVENTURE!
LEGO NINJAGO
COMET CRISIS
GREG FARSHTEY
JOLYON YATES
PAPERCUTZ
LEGO NINJAGO #11